HOOD SUPREME 2

MZ. LADY P

Hood Supreme

Copyright © 2020 by Mz. Lady P
Published by Mz. Lady P

This is a work of fiction. Any references or similarities to actual events, real people, living or dead, or to the real locals intended to give the novel a sense of reality. Any similarity in other names, characters, places, and incidents are entirely coincidental.

PREVIOUSLY IN HOOD SUPREME
MIYANI

I had been numb since hearing the deafening gunshot. Never did I imagine I would see my sister unconscious and bloody. We had been at the hospital all night, and she was in surgery. I was getting more and more worried with each passing minute. The surgeon promised that the surgery would be about four hours. It's been about six now. Usually, when they take that long, it's not good.

"Are you okay, Miyani?" Gianna asked as G basically forced me to allow her on my lap. I hugged her tight as she melted into me. She was obviously tired as she laid her head on my shoulder.

"Yeah, I'm okay. Are you okay?"

"No. I'm not okay. Actually, I'm sad because you're being mean to daddy." I held in my laugh hearing this little con artist.

Looking across the room at G, I rolled my eyes. I'm so mad at this nigga that I want to fight him. He should have told me about his business dealings with my father. I deserved the right to choose if I wanted to continue fucking with him. Besides that, I'm just mad that he made me fall in love with him.

"I'm sorry I've been mean to your daddy." She had a couple of hairs out of place, so I started to fix her pigtails as we sat.

"Are you sorry for being mean to me?" she asked, and now she had my full attention. What was this little girl up to? For her to be so damn young, she was definitely smart. I mean, she does have that damn Alexander blood.

I just shook my head at Ms. Gladys. She was the biggest con artist of them all. They were all huddled up and plotting. I could feel the shit. Prada had to go down to the police station for questioning. Not only did that crazy ass bitch shoot my sister, but she also tried to kill herself.

Unfortunately, the bitch didn't die. She better hope my sister makes it. If she doesn't, I swear I'm going to kill that crazy bitch myself. This shit is so crazy. I'm trying my best not to lose my mind behind this shit. I have no idea what I'm going to do if Gavin dies on me. The relationship with my parents is definitely over. She's all that have in this world. Shaking the negative thoughts from my mind, I gave G a once-over.

Why the fuck this nigga got on them gray joggers, and I'm mad at his ass? I thought to myself before focusing back on Gianna.

"I haven't been mad at you."

"Then why haven't you came and played with me. I haven't been going to do ballet. My daddy said that you were sick, but I didn't believe him."

In that moment, I realized just how much my presence was essential to her. My emotions got the best of me, so I hugged her tight and apologized.

"I'm so sorry. I've been mean to you. Do you forgive me?"

"Yes, I forgive you."

Gianna kissed me on the jaw and hugged me tightly. It's crazy how a kid has the ability to make a grown-up feel better. Looking down at my phone, I realized another hour had passed.

"Come on. Let's go see if the nurse has any news on my sister." Gianna and I walked hand in hand over to the nurse's station.

"They're still in surgery. I promise as soon as they're done, the doctors will come out and talk to you all." Before I could even ask her anything, the nurse stopped me with this same bullshit ass line. I was so damn frustrated I didn't know what to do.

Walking back over to my seat, I plopped down in defeat and started crying my eyes out.

"Come on now, beautiful. Don't do that. Gavin is strong. She's going to be just fine." G wrapped his arms around, and all I could do was cry. I had become overwhelmed with everything that was going on. My heart was aching behind my sister, my parents, and this nigga Givenchy Alexander.

"Why is all of this happening to me, G?"

"Shhh! Stop that crying. Everything will be okay. Everything is going to be just fine. Gavin is going to be just fine. You and I are going to be just fine. Yeah, we're going through a rough patch, but it ain't shit we can't handle. Yeah, we haven't known each other for long, but the chemistry is undeniable. On some real shit, I had no idea I would fall in love with you. For years, there's only been one lady that had my heart. My daughter is my world. To see her so happy to have you apart of our world, let's me know you're the one. Miyani baby, you just have to have faith that this love thing we have will prevail. Stop crying and let me see that beautiful smile I've fallen in love with."

G lifted my head and started wiping the tears from my face. It was hard not to melt into him at this point. Those soft hands and his warm embrace was more than enough to make me forgive him. The words he spoke didn't hurt either

"Are you sure about all of that? I'm sure there will always be drama when it comes to my family and your family. I can't spend my life dealing with that shit. I want a normal life, Givenchy."

"Nothing about either of us is normal. My family engages in criminal activities, and your family uses politics as a front for their criminal activities. No matter what my family or your family does, it doesn't change who Miyani Alexander is."

"Did you just give me your last name without a ring?"

"Hell yeah, I have to put it out in the atmosphere so that it can manifest itself first. I love you beautiful, and I have big plans for us." We exchanged a passionate kiss and became lost in each other.

The sound of someone clearing their throat caught both of our attention.

"I know this got to be a fucking joke!" G said as he quickly stood to his feet.

Snaking my neck around him, I was able to see a woman flashing her badge. In the distance, I saw nothing but uniformed police officers and detectives.

"Hello to you too, Givenchy, it's been a long time."

"Really, India? You're a fucking cop." Hearing him say the name India made me give them my full attention. This was not Gianna's mother standing in front of me.

"You rat ass bitch! I should have killed your ass the moment my grandson brought you home. Remember, I told you the bitch tried too hard to fit in!"

"Yeah, you said that shit Granny! Come on. Put the cuffs

on, hoe! We'll be out this bitch in no time!" Fendi held his hands out as a detective quickly placed the cuffs on him.

Fear and shock washed all over me as I watched them place Ms. Gladys in handcuffs a well. Turning my attention back to G, I couldn't help but cry. He was being arrested and read his rights.

"Daddyyyyyy! Let my daddy go!" Gianna broke away from me and started hitting and kicking the officer.

"Really, bitch? You would do this in front of your own daughter." G's face was so twisted up as he gritted his teeth at her.

I quickly grabbed Gianna and held her tight as I could. Both of our asses were crying now.

"Cut that crying out! Chin up and chest the fuck out! Take care of her until I touch down, okay! Promise me you won't let shit happen to my daughter!"

"I promise."

"Don't worry, Miyani. This will all be over soon," Ms. Gladys said as she winked her eye at me.

One by one, they were all led out of the emergency room in handcuffs. All I could do was put my hands down in my hands.

"You see, it's like I said. That shit wouldn't last. It was over quicker than you thought, huh? You're sitting your pitiful ass out here crying over him. Your sister is back there fighting for her life behind his worthless ass brother. She still has hope, but your ass is too far gone now. That nigga got you on babysitting duty while he does a bid. By the way, that nice lady that arrested him is her mother. I suggest you don't get too attached to her. India is definitely coming for what's hers." My mother winked her eye and walked away like it was nothing.

The whole vibe was different coming from her. How

does she even know G's baby momma? This shit is fucked up all the way around. Somebody needed to wake me the fuck up because this shit was beyond me.

~

Two Weeks Later

By the grace of God, Gavin had pulled through. The bullet missed her heart by inches and lodged in her back. Her surgery took longer because her lungs had collapsed. Surprisingly, she was up and walking around like it was nothing. I personally thought she was trying to do too much, but she refused to lie around.

G, Prada, and Fendi were all still locked up. Ms. Gladys got out a couple of days ago. Much to our dismay, we were lying low in this big ass house close to the Indiana border. Why Ms. Gladys felt the need for us to stay with her, we will never understand.

The paternity results had come back, and Fendi was definitely Chyna's father, well, Chanel. When he got word that the tests came back positive, he had her name changed to Chanel Alexander. That man had already put his foot down and said Dream was not to leave his home. Usually, she would be talking all types of shit, but this time she wasn't. That let me know it was more to them than she had elaborated to me. I knew in due time, it will tell, though. I was so happy for her. Hell, I was delighted for Gavin too. Carlo really let the divorce go through and gave up his parental rights to CJ. Prada's nutty ass had scared the shit out of that coward ass nigga.

Looking down at my phone, I made sure my ringer was on. G would be calling at any moment. I couldn't wait to hear his voice. It was hard not knowing what was going to happen, but I was willing to wait it out, not to mention take care of Gianna as well. I didn't give a fuck about who her mother was. I promised G to protect her, and that's exactly what I was going to do

"Come on in here. I need to talk to y'all!" Ms. Gladys yelled from her office.

"What the hell her busy ass wants now? Did you know there is nothing but bricks of coke in the damn wine cellar? I went down there looking for some damn pink Moscato and damn near caught a contact of that shit. I'm telling y'all we done got mixed up in some cartel shit," Dream said as she bounced her daughter on her knee.

"At least you stumbled upon the drugs. Imagine falling through a damn secret door in the wall with nothing but assault rifles and shit. I saw a fucking rocket launcher. Fuck the cartel! We're dealing with the damn Taliban," Gavin added.

I held in my laugh listening to them. Both of them would shit bricks if I told them that Ms. Gladys' she shed was really a damn torture chamber.

"Come on in here and sit down. I have something for you girls." Ms. Gladys handed each one of us a Harry Winston necklace box.

We all opened them and were surprised seeing we all had a diamond-encrusted money sign chain, which were the same chains everyone with Team Supreme rocked.

"What is this for?" I asked.

"Each of you girls is sitting here because you are near and dear to my grandsons. I've never liked to share my boys with anyone. Ms. Gladys don't trust bitches with my babies. Givenchy, Prada, and Fendi are my most prized possessions. I've raised them to stand their ground, make money, and murder every motherfucking thing moving. You see, right now, they have to sit down for a minute. Regardless of that, there is still money to be made. A man is nothing without the woman who stands beside him. This is the time for you girls to shine and show these motherfuckers you're not the weak woman they think you are. Before we go any further, are you riding with Team Supreme or not?"

For a minute, all of our asses were quiet. I knew G would want me to ride for him so I decided to be all in.

"I'm down," I stated proudly.

"If Miyani's in, then we're in. Right, Gavin?" Dream asked.

"Absolutely. I owe Prada my life, and I'll do anything to help him.

"I'm glad to hear you ladies say that. Welcome to Team Supreme. Ms. Gladys is about to teach y'all the game, and I hope you girls can catch on quick.

Gavin, you now handle all of Prada's pickups and drop-offs. Dream, you now handle rent collections at all of our rental spaces. Miyani, my love, you are the brains of the operation. Your job is the toughest, but I know you can pull it off. It's your job to ensure that Dream and Gavin handle shit accordingly. Don't worry. You'll have Butta, Gunna, and Nettie there if you need them. However, I want the streets to know who the fuck the ladies of Team Supreme are. Put my grandbabies to bed and meet me down in the basement. The first thing I need to teach you is how to shoot. You have to be ready to lay a motherfucker down without hesitation."

"Do you think they will be mad if they find out what we're doing?" I just had to ask.

"Miyani, my darling. Each of you has been strategically handpicked for this. Trust me. They are waiting for my reports back on how good you're running things. Welcome to Team Supreme ladies."

One by one, she placed the gold diamond chains on our necks.

My phone began to ring. It was G. I knew from the number that flashed across the screen. Not hesitating, I quickly answered.

"Chin up and chest the fuck out. You're the boss of this shit now, beautiful."

1

GIVENCHY

Eight months have passed since these cracker motherfuckers locked us up. Being held without a bond was starting to get to a nigga. These people need to figure out what the fuck they're going to do so I could know who needs to get killed first. One thing these motherfuckers got to know is that Team Supreme will never do life in prison.

Right now, we're just chilling and running shit from behind the wall. A nigga was counting his blessings every day for Miyani. My baby had taken over like a mother-fucking boss. Gone was the shy, timid Miyani. My beautiful had been sitting at the roundtable with bosses from all over making deals and holding court. She had definitely made daddy proud. I couldn't wait to get up out this jam and spoil her ass rotten.

Just thinking about Miyani had me stroking my dick. The thought of her fat ass pussy gripping this dick had me bussing nuts back-to-back. Thank God, I was in a cell alone. I had forbidden her to come and see me. The last thing I needed was to see her crying and upset. The last thing she needs is to be upset. At eight months pregnant, the last thing she needs is stress. It's enough she's still been out handling business affairs for me. I had sent word about a month ago for her to stop and let my granny handle my shit.

Learning that Miyani has still been sitting in on meetings and doing pickups had me livid. Yes, I thrusted her into the role of boss, but it was at my discretion. Now that she is damn near ready to give birth to my son, she needs to chill the fuck out.

Besides dealing with Miyani, I was worried about Gianna. Her bitch ass momma was fighting for custody of her. Shit was not looking good on my part. With me being in prison, the judge was definitely going to give her to India. I still haven't come to terms with how this bitch had betrayed me. Never did that bitch give off police vibes. When that bitch wanted out, I thought it was because she didn't want to be a mother, but all along the bitch dipped because she was an undercover narcotics agent. This bitch knew damn near everything about Team Supreme.

I cringed, hearing the tapes from the wires she had worn. During that time, the bitch was in so deep that she was breaking laws with us. The bitch had to walk away before becoming an accomplice because she had done so much illegal shit.

India had literally gone against her superiors and engaged in shit she had no business participating in. Instead of standing in the paint and taking care of her daughter, she dipped. The police ass bitch doesn't deserve to be called a mother. If the courts give my baby to that hoe, I'm going to break out this bitch and murder her myself.

~

"YOU GOT THIRTY MINUTES, ALEXANDER?" the CO said as he led me to a private visiting area.

"Good looking, Lex, you know I got you." She winked at me and walked out of the room.

From the moment we got on the deck, Lex had been making sure we were cool. The best part about this all was that she was Nettie's bitch. She had been smuggling the drugs in for us. We had a nice ass operation going on. Lex was in love with Nettie, so she was willing to do whatever to stay in her good graces. I pray Nettie's dyke ass don't fuck this up. She can't keep a bitch to save her life.

The room door opened just as I was about to grow inpatient. A nigga quickly stood to his feet to have a good ass look at my baby Miyani. My son had her thick and even more beautiful than she already was. Initially, I didn't want her visiting me. That changed after learning that she was still doing business against my orders.

"Damn, beautiful, look at you! Man, I miss your ass so much." I licked my lips in anticipation of feeling her body against mine. It had been a minute since I touched her. It had a nigga feeling like a crybaby ass bitch.

"I miss you too. Don't make me cry, G. I promised myself I wouldn't cry when I came in here." Miyani wrapped her arms around my neck and cried like a baby.

"Shhh! Stop before you stress the baby out. I'm good. Remember what I told you.

"Chin up and chest the fuck out!"

"That's my girl. Come over here and sit on my lap. Tell daddy about your day." I grabbed Miyani by the hand and led her back over to the seat I was previously in.

"G, I'm okay. I would much rather we discuss you. You're more important than what the hell going on with me."

I shook my head listening to Miyani. Sooner or later, she

would realize that I'm a different breed of nigga. I could be on my deathbed and still carry her like she's more important than me. That's how the fuck it should be in any relationship.

"How I'm doing in here is for me to worry about not you. As long as you're holding me down out there, I'm good in here. I'm more worried about my very pregnant woman not listening to me. I know for a fact you got the memo that you're no longer handling things. It's time for you to rest, relax, and prepare to give birth to my son."

"I know that you said that, but it's hard being in that big ass house without you. Yes, Gianna and I keep each other company, but the house is nothing without you. Plus, I have got to get to these city council meetings. The last two, the Chanel House and Supreme Suites, were the topic. The community is trying to petition to halt construction again. We can't afford that. The construction company has been working around the clock to have everything open and ready for tenants no later than the new year. That's two months from now. Right now is not the time. I'll allow Ms. Gladys to do the street shit, but you have to let me handle those properties. It means so much to me to do it, G."

Miyani was damn near pleading to let me do this, and it piqued my interest. I had to know why she was hell-bent on handling it.

"I don't understand why you feel the need to do this. Butta, Nettie, and Gunna could go sit in on the meetings. Why is this so important to you?"

"It's important to me because it's important to you. From the moment we met, you've talked about the importance of opening the Chanel House and Supreme Suites. I want to be instrumental in making sure your mother's legacy is carried on. I've never met her before, but as your woman, I feel like it's my duty to do just that. As far as Nettie, Butta, and Gunna, they would get put the fuck out of there, and you know it. They're too damn ignorant for that setting. Trust me. I got this." Miyani grabbed me by the chin and placed a long deep kiss on my lips.

"I'll agree to let you handle that, but take it easy, Miyani. The first time I get wind that you're doing too much, I'm shutting that shit down."

"Okay. I promise I won't overdo it. Do you think they'll give you all a bond before I give birth? I'm going to be so sad if you're not out to see our son born. All Gianna talks about all day is you coming home and the birth of her brother."

Just to hear how much my family needed me had me fucked up. These crackers needed to do something. Eight months with no bond and barely a case was so fucked up. The judge knew the shit too, but of course, his ass was most likely being paid to keep prolonging the shit.

"Let's not worry about all of that right now. Hopefully, we will get good news at the next court date. Fuck all that, though. I just want to focus on having you here with me at this moment. There is no telling when we will be able to be this close again. Sit up on the table so that I can taste that pretty pink pussy.

"Nah, you sit back and relax. As much as you love for it to be about me, I embrace things being about you. After all, you're the one who's fighting for your freedom. Let me relieve some of your stress."

Miyani pushed me against the table while she took a seat. Without hesitation, she pulled out my hard ass dick and kissed the tip of it before going in. Miyani must have really missed a nigga because she was motor boating the dick like crazy. Her beautiful ass was sucking my dick nasty as fuck. She had me moaning like a bitch as I moved the hair that had fell in her face. I needed to see them juicy ass pretty lips wrapped around my dick. The sight of that alone had a nigga ready to buss all down her throat. I guess she felt me getting ready to buss, so she started sucking hard as fuck. My ass held on to the sides of the table, trying to keep my balance. Miyani had my damn legs feeling like noodles when she was done draining me.

My dick was still hard, and I was so ready to get up in the guts, but I didn't want to hurt the baby.

"I want to feel that pussy, but I'm scared I might fuck around and make you go in labor.

"No, you won't, baby. Just take your time. You can't be trying to go ape shit in the pussy. Give me slow long strokes that touch my inner soul each time you hit it."

Miyani stepped out of her leggings and bent over the chair. Her pussy was dripping wet, and I hadn't even touched it yet. That's the type of shit a nigga loves. As I slid in Miyani's pussy, I knew I needed to get the fuck out of jail. There was no way possible I could go without this on a daily basis.

For the rest of our visit, we fucked in every position that made her comfortable. It was hard having to go back to my cell and she go home alone. In due time we will be reunited and the motherfuckers that trespassed against us had better be ready for war, including her parents. There is no need for me to spare them when they don't give a fuck about her. I want all the smoke behind Miyani.

2

MIYANI

I was so ready to get this baby out of me. It was beyond me how women had multiple children. I see why Kim Kardashian been using surrogates. Ain't nobody got time for this shit. I'm more irritated than ever, and I think it's because G's not here to wait on me hand and foot. This shit sucks without him.

They needed to let him up out of jail so that he could see our son born. I'm almost positive I won't be able to enjoy the idea of bringing my son into this world if his father isn't there to witness it.

Today's visit with G gave me a sense of calmness. It felt good seeing him but even better fucking him. That man was the truth on all levels. A man of his caliber has no business being in jail. He needs to be out in these streets running shit.

It's crazy how life has changed for me since I met him. There was a point when I wouldn't even look at a drug dealer, but now I'm running his business and carrying his baby. After the shit Noonie did to me, I thought I would never love again. Little did I know his betrayal would land me in the arms of my future husband. There I was thinking my life was over, but in reality, it was just beginning. Grateful is not enough to express how my newfound happiness has me feeling. Getting full custody of Gianna and G getting out of jail is all we need to make our little family complete.

Besides dealing with G's business and him being away, I was still running Tippy Toes Dance studio. Due to being pregnant, I had officially taken my leave. I've hired some of the most amazing dancers and staff to run things in my absence. No matter what I'm doing, I make sure the girls see me at least three times out of the week at their evening practices. I was glad Gianna had become comfortable with the other instructors, especially since she wanted to quit when she realized I wouldn't be teaching her for a while. I needed ballet to be her escape from the things going on around her. Not only was her father who raised her since birth locked up, but the mother who abandoned her had also petitioned for custody. Like this bitch walked out and left her daughter for six years, and now she's back trying to take her away from the only family she knows.

I've been fighting tooth and nail on G's behalf, but the shit is looking bleak. The bitch is a federal agent. That alone has the ball in her court. G being in jail helps her case. Federal agent or not, I refuse just to let her take Gianna. I'll lose my freedom and life before I allow that to happen. It was bad enough the judge required visitations at least one week. Each week I be wanting to beat this bitch the fuck up. I'm not one of those females to be out in the streets fighting, but I'll make an exception for India's ass.

~

"PLEASE DON'T BRING any more shit in this house, Gavin! It's bad enough Ms. Gladys out buying power wheels."

My son's nursery was filled to capacity with all types of shit. I had the nerve to let Ms. Gladys pick the theme for it. She chose a damn zoo theme. Now the nursery is filled with life-size animals that move and shit. My baby is going to wake up scared as fuck sleeping in there. If that wasn't crazy enough, she had already got him his first gun, mind you I'm only eight months pregnant. The lady is too damn much for me. I see why Fendi wants to lock her ass away in a nursing home.

"Girl, bye! I'm buying my nephew whatever the fuck I want."

"Well, keep that shit at your house!" I yelled at Gavin as she carried bags up the stairs.

My ass was laying across the chaise in the living room. My back was hurting me so bad that I couldn't walk up the stairs. I'm so ready to drop this load I don't know what to do.

"What the hell wrong with you?"

"I'm ready to have this baby."

My emotional ass started to cry. That's another reason why I'm ready to have this baby. I'm over all of these mood swings. One minute I'm smiling and the next I'm crying.

"It will be over in no time. Stop all that damn crying. It's depressing me."

"Me too. G needs to hurry up and come home."

"Who you telling? Come on, try not to think about that. Get dressed so we can go out and shop. I need something cute to wear when I finally get to see Prada."

My sister's eyes were lit up like a Christmas tree. She was crazy about Prada's crazy ass. I'm so happy she has found someone who loves her and my nephew the way they deserve. Carlo has been staying away from them, but I don't trust his ass. I feel like he's sitting back somewhere plotting. I'm happy we all know how to shoot now. If that nigga moves the wrong way, I'm definitely going to kill his ass. If he knows like I know, he had better leave Gavin's ass alone. She's no longer the woman who allowed him to put his hands on her. All of a sudden her ass is trigger happy. Doing Prada's collecting has required her to run up on a nigga or two.

"How you feel about being able to see him?"

"Man sis, I'm so excited. Talking to him on the phone twice a day is cool, but it's not enough. I need to lay my eyes on him so that I can know he's really okay.

"I know how you feel. After seeing G, I feel a lot better. At the same time, I can't wait until he gets out. It's going to fuck him up if that bitch gets Gianna."

"I've been telling you we should kill that hoe. We can trunk that police ass bitch and use her for target practice."

"Girl, sit your trigger happy ass down. You know them people got eyes on that hoe. If something happens to that bitch, they're going to put it on G, Prada, and Fendi, so we gone let that bitch make it for now."

"Yeah, you right about that. Look at you being the brains of the operation like ya man." Gavin fell out laughing.

"He did say I was the boss of the shit. You know that means I have to move differently. Just know that we one band one sound around this motherfucker. I'm down for whatever when it comes down to Team Supreme!"

"That's just that on that!" Gavin and I high fived each other and I got up to go to the bathroom. That was another thing about this damn baby. He sat on my bladder all damn day. If I cough or sneeze too hard, I'm for sure to piss on myself.

As soon as I sat down on the toilet, my phone alerted me

of a notification. Looking at the screen, I realized it was a security alert showing and telling me someone was at the front gate. Seeing that it was Dream, I quickly opened the security gate. G had this house locked up like Fort Knox.

After using the bathroom, I headed back out to the living room. Dream was walking back and forth looking frustrated. She was also talking to herself as she paced. The bitch looked crazy as fuck too.

"What the hell wrong with you?"

"I went to see Fendi, and a bitch was there visiting."

"Did Fendi say who the bitch was?"

"Nah, I didn't get to see him. The motherfucker refused my visit. I swear to God I'm going to go ape shit if that nigga is playing with my heart. It's two things I hold dear to me — my daughter and my fucking heart — the two things I can't live without. On my life, I will fuck Fendi up."

"Just calm down and wait until he calls you. I'm sure there is a good explanation." I tried my best to be positive in the situation. Dream's ass needed to calm down before she did something hasty.

"What type of explanation can he come up with, Miyani?"

"I don't want an explanation. However, I do want to give him a taste of his own medicine. I'm about to have his ass sitting in there wondering what I'm out here doing. I'm not answering a call until I get good and motherfucking ready since he wants to have me out here wondering what the fuck is really going on. Fendi got me fucked up. I told the bitch not to play with me from the jump. I'm about to turn all the way up on his ass. I'll talk to y'all later. I have to go get my baby from Ms. Gladys' house. Her ass is over there throwing a fish fry and having a card party."

"Now she knows them kids don't need to be over there.

Come on. We can all go get them together," I said as I stood up and placed my shoes on.

"I see why Prada and Fendi want to lock her ass away. She is such a busy body. Do y'all know I woke up to her in my house cooking breakfast? I told Fendi I almost shot her ass."

We all laughed and headed out of the door. There was no telling what Ms. Gladys' ass was over there doing. She keeps saying that she is retired, but I'm not buying it. Ms. Gladys is definitely not retired. Lately, she's been traveling to Colombia a lot. Ain't shit over there but the cartel. That lady is doing something she ain't got no business, and I know in due time it will come to the light.

~

"It amazes me how you hold him down so well. It reminds me of myself."

I bit down on my lip, trying to control my anger. This bitch India had been following Gianna and me around the mall for the last hour. She got to see Gianna every week so, I don't understand what her purpose of her latest stunt is. I remained composed because I didn't want to expose Gianna to anything, unlike the low-class ass bitch that birthed her. India knows that she shouldn't be doing this, but her goal is to antagonize me.

"I'm nothing like you, sweetie. Please find somebody else to play with, beloved. These hands don't discriminate. Anybody can get it, even a rat ass, police ass, unfit ass bitch like yourself. Don't let this stomach fool you."

"Watch it, bitch! I'm still an officer of the law. That nigga got you feeling yourself. Know and understand. You will never have Givenchy Alexander the way I had him. For all you know, I may be back to take my family back! Once a week visits ain't cutting it."

Before I could respond to this bitch, Gianna ran back over to where we were.

"I'm ready to go, Ma. Oh, hey, Ms. India!" Gianna waved at her, grabbed my hand, and started pulling me away.

I didn't have to respond to the hoe. Hearing her daughter call me ma had hurt the bitch as the fuck it should. She abandoned her daughter and her nigga. Now she thinks she can just pop up and get them back. That shit is not happening. I'm not coming up off either of them peri-odt! That bitch got me so fucked up.

I was so pissed on the way home I was fuming. While I know that I should tell G that bitch was following me, I'm not. He has enough on his plate. I can't wait to give birth to my son. That bitch was cruising for a bruising, and I have every intention of giving her what the fuck she's looking for. I don't give a fuck about her being the police either. Obviously, she doesn't give a fuck either.

ABOUT AN HOUR LATER, I was pulling up to the house. I was instantly irritated looking at Butta and Gunna's ass. They were the true definition of stalkers. I know that they're just doing their job, but I can't seem to get a moment to myself, which was why I snuck past their ass this morning and went to the mall. They went to the club last night, so I knew they were fucked up. Their ass was knocked out sleep in the car outside the house.

"Really, sis?" Gunna asked. I observed Butta's fat ass on the phone. From the looks of his face, I could tell it was G.

"Hell yeah, I wanted to get out and get some air. Gianna and I needed some retail therapy.

"Here, G wants to talk to you." Butta grinned, and I rolled my eyes at his fat ass. He and Gunna started grabbing the bags from the car.

I hurriedly walked inside of the house and to G's office. Since he had been away, it had become my office.

"Hello."

"Good afternoon, beautiful. How is your day going so far?"

"It's going well. How about you?"

"I'm good. How are my kids?"

"They're fine, G."

"Listen, beautiful, don't go out alone again. Okay?"

"Okay, G.

"Hear me, Miyani, and hear me good. That incident that occurred today at the mall is why I want you to be aware of your surroundings, no more going out without someone. Gianna is my most prized possession. I would lose my mind if something happened to her. With everything that's going on, I need you to move smarter. I left you in charge because you are smart. This job requires that common sense is always necessary. Look, I got to go. It's time for count. I'll call you later before Gianna's bedtime."

Givenchy hung up before I could say anything, not that I had anything to say. He had rendered me speechless with his choice of words. The rational part of me knows that he meant no harm. However, the crazy, overthinking part of me was feeling like he was calling me stupid and negligent. It also had me feeling a little left out. Let me find out my unborn child and I aren't his prized possessions as well.

That last line has me coming to my senses. I know that

he loves us. It's just that right now, Gianna's safety is important. Honestly, I did fuck up by going without someone. I know the seriousness of all this shit, but by the same token, I do miss my simple life. Going and coming as I pleased was everything to me. Since I've gotten with G, everything is planned and calculated with so many barriers and boundaries. I love my man, but I miss my free boring ass life. All of this needing security and shit is too damn much for me. It's bad enough he calls himself putting me in charge. How in the hell am I the boss, but I'm getting in trouble with his ass?

Heading back down the stairs where Butta and Gunna were. I found them in the TV room watching the news. My eyes were fixated on the screen. My father had been elected for another term as Mayor of Chicago. Despite the way I feel about him at the moment, I am incredibly proud of him. Growing up, I watched my father work hard. To a certain extent, he deserves this. At the same time, both he and my mother have abused the fuck out of his power, and they don't deserve it. As I watched the screen an eerie feeling came over me. I quickly shook it off because it had my baby kicking like crazy.

"I knew his ass was going to get elected again," Gutta said.

"We should have offed that nigga when we had the chance."

Hearing Butta said that took me aback. For a minute, I was trying to get the words he said to resonate in my mind. In an effort to make sure I heard what he had just said, I cleared my throat, and they both looked like deer in headlights.

"What's up, sis? We didn't see you standing there. Your old man did it again, huh? Call us if you need to go anywhere," he casually said as they both walked out of the door.

I hoped neither of them thought I took offense to what they said. It just feels funny to hear my man's henchman talking about how they should have killed my father. That's a conversation most children never get to hear. The shit was weird to hear though. Outside of everything that has happened, I still don't know the full extent of their business dealings. At this point, I don't even want to know. Sometimes we hate to face the truths that are right in front of our faces. Facades are better because it gets you through the day. I know that eventually, everything will come to light. A bitch is just praying that I have the strength and the heart to get through the shit.

3

DREAM

It was the first of the month and time for me to do the rent pickups. I made sure to grab me a tall ass can of Red Bull to drink as I made my rounds. When I agreed to take on Fendi's business dealings, I never imagined my plate would be so full. Besides handling his properties, I now run his club in his absence. I don't know what I would do without my nanny, Ms. Paulette. She had been helping with my baby Chyna, oops I mean Chanel. When the DNA results came back that Fendi was indeed the father, he demanded her name be changed.

Not only did he start throwing out rules for his daughter, but the nigga was also throwing his weight around with me too. Now, I'm all for the nigga being dominating. However, Fendi is gone have to fall in line and understand that I can't be tamed. I've never been told what to do, so him exercising his power got me feeling some type of way. I'm a minute away from taking my baby and saying fuck him. I didn't sign up for all the bullshit that comes behind fucking with Fendi. I've had to beat up two of his hoes for fucking with me. This nigga Fendi is indeed a ladies man. The shit is out of control, and he's behind the wall, so I could only imagine how shit will be when he gets out.

Going up to the jail and seeing this bitch visiting him had me hot as fuck. If the nigga had accepted my visit, I probably wouldn't be so mad. I've been trying to be as tough as I can with this situation. The shit is hard, though. That bitch hurt my feelings, and it was going to take a lot for me to understand why he handled me like that. Yes, we're still in the place where our relationship is growing. Why he trusts me running his shit, I don't know? I'm glad that he does trust me. Gaining his trust means a lot after everything I did to him. I realize I'm feeling some shit for him I've never felt for a nigga. I knew I was in love with the bitch the moment tears welled up in my eyes. Fendi will definitely see a side of me that he does not want to see if he plays with my heart. He thinks I stole that funky ass three thousand and that ugly ass watch. I'm going to rob his ass blind if I even think he's on bullshit.

Despite being in my feelings, I continued to handle this nigga's business accordingly. Fendi's ass had me handling so much money that it didn't make any sense. At first, the shit was overwhelming, but I learned the ropes in no time. The crazy part about it was that I knew some of the shit he had me doing was illegal. It was as if I eased into boss bitch mode easy. My ass got an adrenaline rush out of this world handing shit for him. Fendi had no clue that he and his crazy ass grandma had created a monster.

Opening the rental box, I grabbed all the payments the tenants had left. Prior to me taking over things, Fendi, Butta, and Gunna went to the tenants' apartments personally collecting rent. That was so damn old school, and I was not about to be going to these folks' houses. Either they could put it in the drop box, or pay it online. It's too many damn buildings and tenants for that. I also appointed a building manager for each property. It made my job a lot easier. Fendi's ass was horrible at keeping up with shit. I had paid damn near a million dollars in only eight months fixing the buildings up.

Fendi had so many damn city citations that it didn't make any sense. It was a good thing I had taken a couple of business courses. I was able to create Excel Spreadsheets that helped me keep up with the books. Placing the vacant apartments on Zillow helped to gain new tenants. The properties were all legit, so I enjoyed putting my all into them. In so little time, I've managed to turn them all around.

Now that damn club is another thing. Fendi was going to have my ass in jail behind this shit. On the surface, it looks like a regular club, but beneath the surface it's a full-blown hoe house. These damn Alexanders had their hands in all types of shit. Now Miyani, Gavin, and my dumb ass are right up in the mix with the bullshit. Getting mixed up with Fendi ain't nothing but the good Lord's Karma behind me stealing that man shit.

"DON'T WALK IN HERE with that stank ass attitude! Why haven't you been answering the phone for my baby Fendi?" I rolled my eyes at Ms. Gladys as I walked inside the house with my daughter. I've been ignoring her and his ass.

"I told you already, Ms. Gladys, Fendi got me fucked up. I'm not talking to him until I get ready to. He should never have refused my visit. I couldn't care less about that hoe being there. That nigga said fuck me, so I'm saying fuck him."

"Oh, it's fuck me! Aye, let me holla at your stanking ass!"

Fendi's voice boomed from the phone in her hand. This old lady had me on speakerphone.

"Really, Ms. Gladys? You could have told me you were on the phone with him."

"That would take all the fun out of him cussing you out. Give me my grandbaby. What's up, Miss C?" She took my daughter from my arms and handed me the phone.

"Just for that, I'm one hundred percent on Fendi's side about putting your old ass in a nursing home." We both laughed, and she walked out of the kitchen.

I took a deep breath before talking to Fendi. This nigga had me somewhat shook at the moment. He was mad as hell at me. I could hear it all in his voice. It had been a week since he last heard from me. If he were out, he probably would be choking my ass out. Since he wasn't, that gave me the green light to get on my tough shit.

"Yeah."

"Don't motherfucking yeah me! Why the fuck wouldn't you answer the phone for the nigga? Don't answer that over the phone. Tell me to my fucking face. Bring your ass down here now. I have a special visit."

Before I could answer, the bitch had hung up the phone. My ass didn't have time to waste. I rushed home and changed into something sexy. A bitch needed to look good as fuck when that nigga laid his eyes on me. I had to do something to divert him from wanting to kill my ass.

I ROLLED my eyes in disgust as the correctional officer rubbed his hands all over me. His fat freaky ass was pissing me off.

"That nigga Alexander is lucky as hell. Look, Staples,

this is like the fourth fine ass female that has come to see this man today."

Feeling him rub his hands across my ass made me move out of his way. He was going too damn far.

"Nah, I think she's like the sixth female to come through here. That's your man Ms. Brooks?" the other correctional officer asked.

"That's none of your business. I'll make sure to let him know you take personal interest in his affairs." I rolled my eyes at their ass and walked into the visiting area. I had calmed down for a minute, but now I was right back pissed. Fendi got a gang of bitches coming to see him. He has me so fucked up.

"Visit for Alexander!" the corrections officer who had just frisked me yelled with a grin on his face. Looking around, I realized that the same bitch that was here the last time stood up.

"Aht, aht! You can sit your ass down and wait until I'm finished."

The bitch looked like she had seen a ghost. She couldn't believe I took her fucking visit. She was waiting first so technically it was her visit. Today would be the day I get locked up. I be damn if I let this shit happen again.

The officers thought this shit was so funny. He couldn't contain his fat ass self as he escorted me to a room. Walking inside, I got wet instantly, staring at my fine, rich ass baby daddy. He was brushing the shit out of his thick waves. The nigga waves looked so good I was getting seasick.

"Fuck you come up here looking like you on the runway for? Them CO's was touching on you?"

"Hell yeah! I liked it too," I stated matter of factly as I sat down. That familiar twitch he made with his mouth let me know he was mad. Good! I'm mad too.

"Don't think I won't smack the fuck outta you caused I'm locked up."

"Don't think I'm afraid to get locked up behind smacking your ass back! Now, who are all these bitches coming up here to see you? It's a bitch out there right now who I'm about to slide when she walks up out this bitch. She's the same bitch that came to see you last week. You requested me to come up here last week and then refused my visit. Let me know now if I have to start offing these hoes, Fendi. I decided I'm not sharing you with nobody — periodt. Tell me all them hoes names right now!"

"Man calm your ass down with all that bullshit. Now listen."

"Aht, aht! Don't do that shit, nigga!"

"Damn, Dream! Do what?"

"Lick your lips. Your ass is not doing shit but marinating the lies about to come out of your mouth. Give the shit to me straight with no chaser."

I know I may be being dramatic. On the other hand, Fendi Alexander is the type of man you let know what it is straight out of the gate so that you can decide the way you want this shit to go. A man of his caliber likes to have his cake and eat it too. He needs to know I'm not the bitch that allows that.

"Your ass is crazy, bro. What the hell have I gotten myself into?" He ran his hand over his face in frustration and leaned back in the seat. Instead of smoothing shit over, I decided to take the shit a step further.

"Guardddddd!" I stood up as if I was getting ready to walk out, but Fendi jumped up and grabbed me.

"Damn, man, I'm sorry. Sit your dramatic ass down so I can tell you what the fuck is going on." He pushed my ass back in the seat and stood over me. He leaned over and whispered in my ear.

"All them bitches are on the payroll. We got this pill party going on in this bitch. You really think I just got hoes coming up here. Any bitch that comes up here to see me is working."

"Is that what I'm doing?"

"Hell, nah! You're not working. You're making sure that our future is secured. Do you actually think I would allow you to smuggle drugs in your pussy?

"I'm doing other things for you. What sets me aside from the girls? How do you know that you can trust me after everything I did?"

The way we started is always in the back of my mind. That part of me that overthinks everything has it set in my mind that Fendi's on some get-back. He doesn't make me feel that way at all. I guess it's my guilty conscience fucking with me.

"I don't even think about that shit, love. Let me tell you why you're in charge of my shit. You know numbers, and you can turn a profit. You're just what a criminal like me needs. That added with the fact that you have given me the best thing a woman could ever give a nigga. Having a daughter gives me the purpose I didn't have before. I'm forever grateful to you. As far as me trusting you, I don't. However, the love I have for you will always make me give you the benefit of the doubt. You're still getting to know me, so I'll give you a pass. At the same time, hold me to a better standard. Don't ever not answer the phone for me like that. At least give a nigga the benefit of the doubt, love."

Fendi pulled me up from the seat and sat down. Pulling me onto his lap, I couldn't help but rub my hands over his head.

This man was so complicated. His words and his actions will have a bitch questioning everything. However, I'm no fool. This nigga is testing me to see if he can trust me. Fendi thinks he is so much smarter than I am. What he needs to know is that learning the male species is my specialty. He can't fuck with me when it comes to matching wits. I'll have his fucking head hurting. Both Fendi and I were too smart for our own good. This whole ego thing between both of us is going to turn into some toxic shit. I can feel it.

He lifted my chin and kissed me on the lips. The nigga thought he was slick. He was trying to charm his sexy ass back into my good graces. I'm not going to lie. The shit was working. He knew I couldn't be mad at his ass for too long.

"How is my princess doing?"

"She's fine with her greedy self. Your grandma be feeding her all types of shit. Ms. Gladys takes her to Popeyes every day for a spicy chicken sandwich."

"Don't be letting her feed my baby that greasy shit. Those folks not clean in them fast food restaurants. I'm going to hire a chef to come and prepare the meals. You eat a lot of junk food and shit that's bad for you. I watched you're eating habits when you were at the house with me. Your ass is gone have high blood pressure if you keep eating like that."

"Your grandma is going to be the one with the high blood pressure if she keeps eating Popeyes every damn day. I would argue with you about the chef, but I know it would be in vain. I promise to slow up with the bad eating habits. Forget all of that. The baby and I are fine. What's important is if you're okay?"

"I'm in jail, love. It ain't a vacation I would like to take. However, I'm in no control of the way these pigs handling my fam and me. Don't worry. We'll be home soon."

"Is there anything you need me to do for you?"

"Yeah, take that shit off." Fendi started pulling at my leather pants.

"We can't. What if somebody walks in?"

"I got this room for an hour, and them niggas know not to come in here. Now shut the fuck up and take that shit off. Give me some that thieving ass pussy!"

"You are not funny, nigga!" I playfully punched him but quickly unbuttoned my sheer blouse. Fendi definitely didn't have to tell me twice. As I removed my clothes, I was mad at myself for dressing up like this. My ass had on leather pants and thigh-high boots. That didn't stop Fendi's freaky ass, though. He helped me come up out of all that shit.

Fendi's dick was bulging out of his prison jumpsuit. My mouth salivated as I observed him unleash the beast. Instead of letting him hop right off in the pussy, I dropped to my knees and started sucking his dick.

Back when I first fucked him, I sucked his dick so good I had his toes curling.

"Mmmmm! I moaned out as I bobbed my head up and down on the dick.

Afterwards, I started to lose my top and go crazy. He had grabbed the back of my head and began to fuck the shit out my throat. With no gag reflex, I was able to take that shit like a porn star. Moments later, he was releasing his seeds down my throat. As I swallowed, I realized this nigga definitely had me in love with him. I had never done shit like this in my life. Then again, I never fucked with other niggas the way I fuck with this man.

"Bend your ass over!"

Before I could fully stand to my feet, Fendi roughly pulled me up. Not hesitating, he slammed me forward on the table and went balls deep without hesitation.

"Fuckkkkkkkk! You bet not give this pussy to nobody!" I was trying to respond, but I couldn't form the words. Fendi was fucking me so roughly I couldn't even breathe properly.

"Tell me this my pussy!"

"This your pussy, Fendiiiiii! I'm about to cum, bae. Don't nut inside of me!" I could feel him swell up inside of me, and sure as shit, he released inside of me.

"Ahhhhhhh! That's some good thieving ass pussy right there."

"Shut up, Fendi! I told you not to nut in me!" I was mad as hell. My baby just turned one, and I was not trying to be pregnant again so soon. Fucking him raw the last time got me pregnant, so I know how this shit is going to go.

"Man, fuck all that. Are you my girl or not?"

"Let's get something straight. I'm nobody's girl. As a matter of fact, I'm a grown ass woman who prefers to be a nigga's ole lady. Real niggas don't play about their ole lady."

"I'm a real ass nigga, and you already know this. I'll call you whatever the fuck you want, but you need to let me know what the fuck it is now!"

"Damn, Fendi! I'm your girl. The crazy part is that you already know this. We already said we were trying the relationship thing out, so I'm lost as to why you're asking me that shit anyway."

"I'm asking your ass that because if that's my pussy, I can nut in my shit. It shouldn't be a fucking problem."

"It's not a problem. I'm just not ready to have a baby so soon. Our daughter just turned one, and going through that pregnancy was rough. I don't think I can handle being pregnant so soon," I talked to him as I placed my clothes back on. His ass needed to understand where I was coming from. My ass was in no mood for that type of pressure. It was bad enough he had me out in these streets acting like a queen pin. I refused to be toting guns and waddling.

"The difference between that pregnancy and this one is that I'm here. That's my son right there." Fendi grabbed me and wrapped his arms around my waist. As I stared into his deep dark eyes, I knew that he was dead ass serious.

"Just a minute ago, you didn't want a girlfriend or kids. Now all of a sudden you're ready for a son?" I asked while wiping specks of my eye glitter from his face.

"That was before I knew what I didn't want was exactly what I needed. Love, I need my own family." He grabbed me by the chin and kissed me passionately.

"Times up, Alexander!"

To hear the guard say that while pounding on the door made my heart sank. I was not ready to go at all. Time went by so fast. It seemed like I had just made it there. Moments later, the guards were walking in. I wanted to cry so bad watching them place Fendi back in the shackles and handcuffs. As bad as I wanted to shed tears, I knew that I couldn't. Fendi needed me to be strong. That weak bitch shit does not cut it with his nutty ass.

"Let's go, ma'am!" a female guard said aggressively.

"I'll call you tonight, love."

"Okay."

Fendi was escorted out first, and then I was escorted out. The bitch that previously waiting to see Fendi was no longer in the visiting area. I didn't have time to worry about that hoe. I needed to get my ass to Walgreens quick. I needed to grab a Plan-B pill. Yeah, I wanted a future with Fendi. However, he wasn't about to have me around this bitch barefoot, pregnant, and waiting on his ass, no sir. If he wants me to bear him more children, he will have to put a ring on it. I'm securing my future the right way.

4

GAVIN

Learning that my father had won the election was bittersweet. On the one hand, I wished I were there to celebrate with him. On the other hand, I wished that he had lost. Being the mayor had him fucked up as a person and a father. Honestly, I wish that we were a normal family. Politics have divided us as a family, and it's sad as hell. Truthfully, I've never felt like we were family. The only thing we all had in common was that we shared blood.

It wasn't until I got to know Ms. Gladys and Prada that I know what family was. They have each other's back no matter what. The way they stand up for each other is amazing to watch. My family has no love within it, and it's sickening. It took for all of this shit to happen for me to really take the blinders off. I'm starting to believe Miyani when she says we don't belong to them.

This damn pregnancy has this girl thinking our ass was kidnapped at birth. At first, I thought she was playing until I realized she was researching our mother. I can't wait until she gives birth to my nephew. This pregnancy has her mean as fuck. I'm so damn happy for my sister, I don't know what to do. She is finally living the life that she deserves. G being away is so hard on Miyani. She puts on a brave face in front of us, but I know she's having a hard time being pregnant, raising Gianna, and running Alexander Enterprises.

At times like this, a girl needs her momma. Unfortunately, the last place our mother wants to be is supportive of her daughters. Since the incident with Prada fucking Carlo up, we haven't spoken to our parents. I would be lying if I said my feelings weren't hurt behind this. It was like one moment we had parents, and the next we didn't. I miss my father more than anything. We've always had a bond. My mother has made sure to ruin that.

Immersing myself into making sure things were straight for Prada kept my mind off the bad stuff. So much had happened to me all at once. Going on the run from Carlo, getting shot, and now running Prada's businesses was a lot to take in. However, I embraced it. All of that shit made me stronger. It was as if I grew the fuck up overnight. Being with Prada showed me the things I lacked as a woman with Carlo. With Prada, I had to step my game all the way up. There was no more room for that weak bitch shit. All of that being afraid of my parents and Carlo was gone. I'll put a bullet in a bitch's head these days behind fucking with me.

The first on my list is that hoe Esha! It's on sight whenever I see that delusional bitch. She escaped from the damn mental hospital and no one knows where she is. Ms. Gladys had taught me how to handle some real artillery, so the bitch has no idea what's in store if she comes fucking with me. I already know the bitch somewhere lurking. That bitch is bitter behind Prada leaving her. She has it in her crazy ass head that Prada left her for me. I know firsthand that nigga left her ass before he and I were a fucking thought.

Lord, I pray that nigga doesn't have me out here crazy shooting bitches. Prada's definitely worth fighting for, so I don't blame the bitch for being crazy behind his ass. At the same time, she had better leave me the fuck alone with her nutty ass. Quiet as it's kept, I need to start looking for her ass to get my lick back. The crazy bitch could have killed me.

Going through things makes you become so fucking tough. After Carlo, I refuse to let anyone play with me on any level. In a matter of eight months, I've gotten the confidence I yearned for all of my life. Sometimes I be thinking if I went from a bad situation to a worse one. Then I remember what Prada said about this new life being a blessing. Lord, knows I needed it behind me due to the things I had endured at the hands of Carlo and my mother.

I never knew how toxic my mother was until she poisoned my sister and me with her venom. I thank God for meeting Ms. Gladys. My life has changed for the better being with the Alexander family. My parents' toxic behavior is no longer my concern.

MY HEART RACED GETTING to the hospital. Miyani called me screaming and hollering through the phone. Her water bag had burst while she was sleeping. I could hear the fear in her voice. It's a wonder my ass wasn't pulled over the way that I was driving.

Ms. Gladys was the first person I saw when I pulled my car up to the valet area. She was smoking a Black and Mild, and all I could do was shake my head. When in the fuck did she start smoking those stanking ass things? I swear this old lady was full of surprises.

After handing the keys to the parking attendant, I

walked over to Ms. Gladys. She was visibly nervous, which was a first. That woman never busses a sweat. Hell, her ass is smiling on all of her mugshots.

"Any word on Miyani?"

"They're trying to see if they can stop the labor, but he's ready to come. I had to leave out of the room. Miyani is acting a fool, and I need to handle some shit. Go ahead and sit with her. I'll be back as soon as I can. Hopefully, the baby marinates until I get back. Dream is already up there with her. I had her placed in a private area with her own staff. I don't trust anyone right now. That's the "golden child" getting ready to be born. Niggas will kill that baby to hurt Givenchy."

I didn't like the look on Ms. Gladys' face when she said that. Like who would want to kill a damn baby? It's hearing shit like that, that scares me. Yes, we did choose to become a part of Team Supreme, but not at the expense of our babies.

When the valet pulled up with her Maybach, she rushed over to it. *What the hell could be more important than being here?* I thought to myself. Ms. Gladys was so damn mysterious. It's like one minute she's a regular pie baking ass grandma. The next, she's a gun-toting granny. The way she hopped in her Maybach let me know she was on a mission.

Without another moment to wait, I walked inside the hospital, got my pass, and headed up to Labor and Delivery. I was getting ready to be an auntie, and I was elated. I wish a bitch would fuck with my nephew or my sister.

When I stepped off the elevator, Butta was the first person I saw.

"Hey, Butta. Why you standing there looking like you scared?"

"Shit! Cause I am. You need to get in there."

"I told his ass to grab some gloves. We're about to deliver

nephew," Gunna said as he started putting on gloves. I couldn't do shit but laugh because Gunna was serious as hell.

"I saw my baby momma, Quita, give birth to our daughter. A nigga still traumatized. Could you get the nurse? I think I'm going to be sick." Butta was too damn big to be acting like this. He was really standing over the garbage as if he was about to throw up.

"Nigga, get your big soft ass over there and sit down!" Nettie yelled as she came out of the room.

"Man, fuck you, Nettie. Your ass is a whole nigga out here with no heart. How in the fuck are you gone judge me?"

"I wish both of y'all shut the fuck up. They asses had been arguing since we got here and I know sis is sick of their ass because I am. Let's go smoke a blunt or something. The doctor said nephew probably wouldn't come until tomorrow anyway. Call us if anything changes. G wants a conference call, so we have to head over to the office. Prada wants to know if Smitty gave you his contributions from the month."

"No. He's had me drive out to his spot three times this week. Each time I got there, he didn't have the full amount. He still owes me ten grand. I've been holding out telling Prada because I don't want him to think I can't handle myself. Next time I go out there, I'm going to make him give me my nigga's money."

Smitty owned a pool hall that operated on the far south side of Chicago. Every month he has to pay to continue to play. Apparently, he thinks shit is sweet with Prada being locked up.

"Word to the wise, never keep anything like this from him. I'll ride out there and get it. Don't worry. I'll let him know what's up. Bring y'all ass on!" Gunna was so mad at

Nettie and Butta it wasn't funny. They all argued while heading towards the elevators.

I took a deep breath before walking inside of Miyani's room. The sound of her fussing made me wish I smoked a blunt before coming.

"It's about time your ass made it. Please get me something to eat. They're saying I can't eat right now. All I want is a triple bacon burger with some chili from Wendy's."

"Please, Mrs. Alexander, calm down. You're stressing the baby out. I can't allow you to eat anything. There is a possibility you may need a C-section. All she can have is some ice chips." The nurse was older and mean. Miyani was assed out. That lady was not about to let her eat, and neither was I.

Hearing Miyani was about to have a C-section had me concerned. This was her first baby, and this shit was about to be so painful for. I was the same way with CJ. That's why I'm afraid to have another baby. The healing process was a bitch.

"Fuck you and them ice chips! Please, Gavin, make them feed me." Miyani was really sitting up in bed crying because she couldn't eat.

"Look, you're making the baby's heart beat too fast. Calm down. You'll be able to eat whatever you want after you give birth. Please stop giving this lady a hard ass time."

"I want G!"

My heart sank because Miyani put the sheet to hide her face. I quickly wrapped my arms around her and let her get it out. My sister was crying so badly that she could barely breathe. The monitor started to go crazy.

"Mrs. Alexander, please stop crying and upsetting the baby. I promise everything is going to be okay." As she started fixing the monitors on her stomach, Dream walked in with her phone up to her ear.

"Stop all that crying right now before my god baby come out fucked up! Here get this phone. It's ya baby daddy, hoe!" The nurse couldn't help but laugh at Dream's ignorant ass. Miyani wiped her face with her gown and grabbed the phone.

"Put it on speakerphone too. He's about to get on your crybaby ass."

"Keep it up, and you won't be my baby's god momma."

"Girl, bye! I don't want to be Chanel's momma, so no love will be lost. Now put it on speakerphone."

"Bitch, your ass is crazy." I laughed as she sat next to me. "Hello."

"What's up, beautiful? How are you feeling?"

"I'm hungry, and they won't let me eat. This baby is coming a month early, You're not here, and my nurse is mean to me. Gavin is not helping me, and Dream is being a bitch!"

I couldn't believe this girl right now. She was really trying to make G think we were doing something to her.

"Let the nurse Mama Bell know I said give my baby whatever the fuck she wants. Yo, Gavin, help my baby out. Stop being a bitch, Dream. You feel better, beautiful?"

"Yes, I do. I miss you so much. Why can't they do something to stop the labor?"

"Stop crying. That's not the way that it works and you know that. You're about to give birth to the greatest that will ever do this shit. Wipe your face and boss up. It's time to bring a king into the world. He comes from my loins, but inside of him sits your heart and soul. What did I tell you, Miyani?"

"Chin up and chest the fuck out!"

"In that order. Now, the next time I call I want to speak to the mother of my son, okay?"

"Yes, G!"

"I love you, Miyani Alexander."

"I love you too."

It was crazy watching Miyani's mood change in a manner of minutes.

"Bitch, that nigga got your ass gone. I love it. Prada needs to step his damn game up. He's so damn disrespectful. G ass is such a damn gentleman."

"Who you telling? Fendi doesn't have a romantic bone in his body with his psycho ass. Don't think we missed him calling you Miyani Alexander. Let me find out y'all got married on the low without telling us." Dream was asking the very thing that I was thinking.

"He said he's getting prepared for when he makes me his wife."

"You got you a good man on your hands, baby. He reminds me so much of his momma it doesn't make any sense." The nurse began to read the paper to see how often the contractions were coming.

"You know Givenchy?" Miyani asked.

"I just happened to assist in his birth. Ms. Chanel loved me so much she made me godmother to that child. Yes, dear, I know what I'm talking about. You have you a good man on your hands. Now settle down. Your blood pressure is a little high, and it concerns me. Y'all keep her calm I'm going to go and report to her doctor. Do not sneak her any food, and I mean it." Nurse Bell pointed her finger at us as if we were children before walking out of the door.

"This damn family knows everybody. How in the hell they momma just made that damn stranger Givenchy's godmother? I bet her ass is running a cartel up out this damn hospital. I'm telling y'all we need to start paying attention to everybody that we come in contact with. We love them niggas, but we have to run this shit right. After you have this baby and heal up, we're hitting the fucking ground running."

"I most definitely agree with you. Their ass is so secretive. At the same time, I know that there are certain things they keep a secret for the sake of our safety."

Dream ass was absolutely right. We need to pay attention to everything.

"Can we talk about this shit later? In case y'all forgot my ass over here in labor." Miyani gripped the bed rail and braced herself as a contraction passed.

"Nah, hoe! Take that pain just like you took that dick!" Dream said, and we all started laughing. Miyani managed to let out a slight laugh despite the pain.

A text came through to the phone, and I couldn't contain myself. I showed Dream and I could tell she was feeling some type of way as well. Miyani needed to hurry up and have this baby. Shit was definitely shifting in the atmosphere for all of us. This baby was so damn special. He was our good luck charm and no one could tell me differently.

5

—————

GIVENCHY

"What the fuck is going on, bro?" Fendi had asked me for the one-hundredth time.

I was still trying to find out myself. He, Prada, and I were being processed out. We had no fucking idea what was going on. This shit could be a setup, and I couldn't wait to get in contact with our lawyer.

"I don't care what the fuck is going on. I just need to get the fuck out of here."

Prada's ass was ready to get the hell out of here. Hell, we all were. It had been eight months, and Miyani was about to give birth to my son. I prayed my little man waited until his pops could get there.

"All I want to do is eat some of grandma's cooking," Fendi said.

We all couldn't wait to fuck some of her good ass food up. She was definitely going to have a feast waiting on us. Hell, knowing her, she may be the reason we're up out this jam. If that's the truth, then that means she has probably made a deal that requires us to do some off the wall ass shit.

About two hours later, we had been processed

completely. I reached out to Gavin and Dream letting them know not to say anything to Miyani. A nigga wanted to surprise her spoil ass. She was definitely cutting up because they won't give her what she wants. I've created a monster, and I know that it will come back to bite me in the ass. Now, I have two women that have me wrapped around their finger.

"It's about time y'all ass made it here. You've been out for two hours."

Ms. Gladys was sitting in Team Supreme Headquarters with the judge who was over our case. I should have known this woman had a trick up her sleeve. Butta, Gunna, and Nettie were also in the room. The looks on their face showed that they were just as lost as we were.

"We had to wash our asses and change. What the hell is going on, grandma? I can't be here too long. Miyani needs me at the hospital."

"I know that, Givenchy. That's why if y'all shut the fuck up and let me speak, we can all head to the hospital. I'm not about to miss my great-grandson coming into this world."

"Gangsta granny strikes again." Fendi shook his head and took his usual seat.

"Fendi, please don't make me beat your ass. Come on in here and sit. We have some shit to discuss."

"Fuck you doing here, Your Honor?" Prada asked with a smirk as he sat down.

Before I could listen to whatever bullshit they were about to tell us I needed a drink. Grabbing my bottle of D'ussé, I knocked back two shots and sat behind my desk.

"He's here because he needs us to do a hit for him,"

Grandma Gladys spoke casually as she knocked back a shot of Jameson.

"Let me guess. That's the reason we're out, huh?"

"Yes, Mr. Alexander. When your case landed in my lap, I decided to do some research. What I learned was very intriguing. Your street credentials are unheard of by any other cartel."

"Objection! Your Honor, I resent you for making such a crazy accusation!" Prada yelled as he banged on the table. This nigga is a damn fool. He was literally acting as if he was a damn lawyer, and we were in the courtroom.

"Yeah, I object too. If it pleases the court, we would like that shit struck from the record," Fendi added.

Both of these niggas played entirely too much. The shit was funny, though. Hell, Judge Akron couldn't contain his laughter either.

"You're right. I apologize for making that false accusation. Please forgive me. Now, after looking at your case, I decided to have it thrown out due to loopholes. That added with knowing people in high places that also wants what I want."

"Talk to me. Stop bullshitting. Who the fuck do you want murked?" I was growing impatient. All a nigga wanted to do was get to the hospital and surprise Miyani.

"I want you to assassinate the governor of Illinois."

"You're fucking with us, right?" Gunna asked while laughing. I had to take a real good look at him to make sure the judge was serious. His face told me that he was.

"Assassinate is a strong ass word, Your Honor," Fendi commented.

"Assassinate sounds better to me than murder." Prada added.

"How do we know this isn't a setup? For all we know

your ass is setting up to go down for the rest of our lives. As far as I'm concerned, we can head right back to jail. This shit is beyond me. We've sat behind the wall for eight damn months, and you've been over our case from the jump. Why are you now just throwing the shit out?" I needed to know. There was so much more than our street credentials and loopholes in the case that swayed him.

"I'm your grandfather. Your mother, Chanel, was my daughter."

"Listen, it's been years since I saw Joseph. We both grew up in Meridian, Mississippi. When I got pregnant with Chanel, I skipped town and never talked to him again. It wasn't until your first court date that I realized who he was. Don't be mad at him. He had no idea about Chanel being his. As far as him just not getting you out, that was my doing. We needed to learn who all the key players are in the case against us. With Joseph's connections, I've learned so much."

"I can't deal with this right now. Let's meet up and discuss this shit later this week. Miyani needs me." I didn't wait to hear anything from anyone. Right now, I needed to be with the family I was creating. The one I was born into was giving me hell at the moment.

Walking out of the warehouse, I could hear Prada and Fendi asking questions, which was cool. Without a doubt, we were going to do the hit. I just wasn't about to jump on the bandwagon and be all for it. I needed to do my research on Judge Akron's ass first. Heading to the hospital, I placed a call to my private investigator regarding Judge Joseph Akron. I was going to murk his ass if he was on bullshit long lost grandfather or not. It was obvious my grandmother was still a little sweet on his ass. Never in the history of us being Team Supreme have I ever saw her so adamant about doing some shit. I'm grateful he pulled strings to get us out, but at the same time, I'm worried about what it will cost us in the long run.

MY YOUNG KING Givenchy Alexander Jr. had finally graced this cruel world with his presence. He had taken his poor momma through it, but it was worth it in the end. Just being able to be there and witness it had me feeling good as fuck. A nigga didn't give a fuck about the problems that plagued me in the streets. Staring at my son made all that shit seem like small shit to a giant. I had made it out just in time to see him born, and that meant the world to me. As soon as I made it to the hospital, Miyani was getting ready to push.

The whole family, along with Team Supreme, was outside of the nursery looking at my son.

"That little nigga's hair is long as hell," Prada said.

"That's exactly how G's hair was when he was born. It was so pretty and thick. You could put it in a ponytail. My God, he's handsome."

"Yes, he is, Ms. Gladys. My nephew is going to be a heartbreaker."

"I can't wait until Miyani wakes up and sees him. She's going to be so in love," Dream added.

I was happy that Miyani and Gavin were here from the moment she went into labor. As much of a brave front she puts on, I know she wishes that she was on good terms with her fucked-up parents.

"Congratulations, big bro. We're about to head out so that you and Miyani can have some time alone. We'll get up tomorrow and handle this business," Fendi said as we dapped it up. I did the same with Prada and hugged the girls before they all left the nursery. It was now just my grandma and I left standing there looking at my son.

"You know I would never have you boys do anything I think would fuck you up in the long run."

"I know you wouldn't. Grandma, you know we're going to do whatever it is you tell us to do. At the same time, if you're feeling something for that nigga don't let it blind your judgment. We're Team Supreme, remember that." I kissed her on the cheek while wrapping my arm around her.

"Listen to you trying to teach me the game. Nigga, I created the game. We're going to handle that business for the judge. Let me handle his ass, though. Congratulations on your new bundle of joy. You need to spend this week with Miyani and the kids, and then it's back to business. We have an empire to run." She kissed me on the cheek and walked her conniving old ass off.

I love my grandma, but it's always some shit going on with her behind the scenes. I should have listened to Fendi and Prada a long time ago and put her ass in the nursing home.

~

"He is so perfect, G."

"Just like his momma. I love you so much." I kissed both Miyani and our son on the forehead.

Miyani finally woke up and was breastfeeding our son. I pulled the recliner closer to the hospital bed so that I could be close to them.

"I love you too. I'm so happy you're home. Do you still have to fight the case?"

"Let's not worry about that right now. You just gave birth to my son. A nigga would much rather discuss his college fund or some shit." She was worried about the wrong thing at the moment.

"I'm sorry. I just want you to stay out. My ass never wants to sit in a courtroom again."

"Trust me. I don't want to either. However, in the line of work I'm in, sitting in the courtroom comes with the territory. As I said, don't worry. I'm going to do everything in my power to stay out that motherfucker."

"Okay, G. Where's Gianna? I thought I was going to be able to see her today. Did Ms. Gladys pick her up from India like she was supposed to?"

"Something came up. After I leave here, I'm going to grab her. India and I have unfinished business."

"Y'all don't have unfinished business. Send somebody else to get Gianna." Miyani rolled her eyes so hard I thought they would get stuck. I had to hold my laugh in because my baby was jealous.

"Don't be like that, beautiful. India is my enemy, and you're my wife. There is no competition. There is no comparison. Do you trust me?"

"It's not you that I don't trust. That bitch wants you back, Givenchy. Trust me. She doesn't care about that police shit. She's still in love with you and is back for a reason."

"I don't trust her, either. However, we need to have a discussion. Gianna is the topic, not to mention the fact that she's a rat. The last thing I want to do is talk to the bitch, but a sit-down is a must. You have nothing to worry about."

"I'm not worried at all."

There she was again in her feelings. I couldn't argue with her right now. She was emotional and thinking crazy. This would be one of those things that become a test. Miyani has to see the bigger picture here, not the picture that makes her think I will cheat on her with a bitch.

"The doctor said we could head home tomorrow. I'm so happy. I hate being in this hospital. Plus, I miss Gianna. Make sure you let her FaceTime me when you pick her up."

"I promise I will as soon as I pick her up. Send me a text and let me know what I need to bring back. I love you, beautiful." I kissed Miyani on the lips and made sure to kiss my son on the forehead.

"I love you more, G." We kissed one last time before I walked out of the room.

She was definitely in her feelings about me meeting up with India. Miyani had to know that the bitch and I would have to cross paths eventually. After all, the bitch is trying to take my daughter. She just didn't anticipate me getting out so early. The bitch got a problem on her hands now.

"You can't bring that gun in here, Mr. Alexander!"

"I can do any motherfucking thing I want to do. My shit is registered already. Ain't that right, India? Tell your minions to move the fuck around. You and I both know I don't like niggas touching me. Where the fuck is my daughter, you rat ass bitch?"

If this hoe thought that I was coming here on some nice shit, she had me fucked up! This police ass is nigga telling me I can't bring a gun in her crib, but my shit registered in her name. All my guns were in the hoe's name. The look on her face lets me know she forgot.

Looking around at all of her security and the crib India was set up in sent my antennas up. She couldn't afford this on a federal agent's salary. She was looking like the India I remember the more I stared at her, rocking nothing but designer and iced the fuck out. What federal agent you know dresses like that? Yeah, this hoe was moving weight on the low.

"Fall back, Jax. I'll call you if I need you."

"Yeah, fall back or get fucked up! Now, what's good with ya, pussy ass hoe!"

"Is that how you talk to that bitch?"

"Don't ever disrespect her again. Your beef is not with Miyani. Bitch, it's with me! Don't ever follow her again or come at her on no hoe shit. Rat ass, pig ass bitch I'll murk ya and gladly do time behind her."

"Bad word, daddy!" Gianna rushed toward me, and I quickly pulled her in my arms.

"Go back over there and put your headphones on. Let me finish talking to India!" I kissed Gianna on the cheek and rushed back over to the table where she was previously sitting.

This bitch India pulled out a blunt and flamed it up. I couldn't believe this shit. She was definitely on bullshit.

"I remember you were the same way about me, always so territorial about your baby India. It's like you went out and found you a mini-me. The funny thing about that is she's far from being me. That ballerina is all bark and no bite. Oh yeah, I don't appreciate her telling my daughter to call her momma."

Yeah, this hoe was delusional. Clearly, the bitch is out of touch with reality.

"Your ass is smoking dick if you consider your weak ass a mother. Did you forget you gave birth to Gianna and abandoned her? She doesn't have to call you shit because she doesn't know your ass."

"Be that as it may, the fact remains the same. She came out of my pussy. The last thing I wanted to do was leave the love of my life and our daughter. It was either stay and go to prison or leave to keep everyone out of jail. That day I left the hospital, they left me no choice. They were threatening me with taking Gianna from us. I talked to my superiors before I went into labor. She told me that the case was over, and they had sufficient evidence. My services were no longer needed. They snatched me out of the hospital and sent me off to Virginia.

I tried going on with my life, but of course, when the government calls, it's a must you answer. Apparently, your father is out of prison and back in the drug game, courtesy of Team Supreme. The shock in your eyes tells me you have no idea. You may want to holla at Fendi and see what's good with that. No need to thank me for the intel. It's the least I could do. By the way, I'm no longer a federal agent. Get used to seeing this face. I'm back in Chicago to stay. I have unfinished business here."

"Handle your shit, but don't forget who runs this city. Nothing moves in and nothing moves out unless I say so. Let's go, Gianna!"

Getting the fuck out of there was necessary. I was a minute away from choking this bitch. All of that talking she was doing did nothing but make me want to play nice with the bitch. Yeah, she wanted my attention, and she definitely has it.

On the ride home, I couldn't help but think about the shit India said about Fendi. I'm going to fuck that nigga up if he making moves and not informing us. The fucked-up part about it is that he's doing shit with Slim. He knows how we feel about that motherfucker. To keep this shit a secret makes me wonder what the fuck else he keeping from me. I'm getting hit with revelations from all angles, and the shit not sitting right with me. In one day, I found out my bitch ass father was out of prison, and I had a long last grandfather.

"Are you home to stay, daddy?"

"Yes, I am baby. I'm so sorry I had to leave you. Daddy missed you so much." Gianna was so excited in the backseat she couldn't contain herself.

"It's okay. Miyani and I held it down for you, daddy. Can we please go to the hospital and see my brother?" I held in my laugh hearing her talking about holding it down.

"Miyani and your brother come home tomorrow. Let's go shopping and get them some gifts."

"Yayyyyy shopping!" Nothing made my daughter happier than shopping. It felt good to get out and spend some time with my family.

The shit was about to be short-lived cause things were about to get funky for Team Supreme. I need my eyes in the streets, on my money, and on my product. Fendi had better have a good fucking explanation as to why he doing side deals with the enemy.

6

———

PRADA

I t felt good as fuck to be home with my baby Gavin. Fucking with her was like a breath of fresh air. She knew how to please a nigga on all levels without being asked. Each and every time I come home to dinner, her waiting for me is everything. No one has ever catered to me like Gavin does but my grandma. That's how I know I love and want to be with her. After all, she did take a bullet from a nigga.

I still can't believe they let Esha's ass escape. There is no telling where she could be. Her fat ass grandma had up and moved all of a sudden. Without a doubt, they're together. I'm going to find that bitch and murk her if it's the last thing I do.

We were all taking a couple of days off before we hit the streets, which was cool with me. A nigga needed all the rest I could get. There was no telling when this shit would be over.

"Since when you start smoking weed?" I asked Gavin as we sat up in bed chilling and watching *Power*.

"Dream is such as badass influence. When you first got

locked up, it was hard for me to sleep in this big ass house by myself. She told me it would help me sleep. Now, I smoke before breakfast, for lunch, after dinner, and anytime I get the urge to. The shit is beyond me."

"I love that you smoke. The shit makes you relaxed. When I first met you, your ass was uptight like a motherfucker. I didn't like your ass at all."

"Now look at you, all in love and eating my ass!"

"I plan on eating that motherfucker every chance I get."

A nigga was dead ass serious too. Eating pussy has never been something I just did. Gavin's shit was different, though. Hell, everything about Gavin is different. After hitting the blunt a couple of more times, I pulled her on top of me.

"My pussy is hurting, Prada! I don't think I can fuck again. Let me get some rest, and then I'll be ready to go again."

I couldn't do shit but laugh. From the moment I touched down, we had been fucking like rabbits. My goal was to get her pregnant. A nigga definitely wanted to have a big ass family with her. Sometimes I sit back and watch how good of a mother she is to her son. Gavin literally juggles motherhood and handling shit for me like a boss. I can't thank my grandma enough for rescuing her. A nigga like Carlo didn't deserve this type of woman. She's a different breed, and he knew nothing about handling her.

"Let me kiss it and make it feel better."

"Nah, I'm not falling for that trick again. Plus, I have to make these runs with your grandmother. I promise we can fuck all you want tonight. Right now, I'm about to soak in the tub and get dressed. Are you sure you don't want me to cook tonight?"

"Nah, I have to meet up at the club with the crew. It's

Nettie's birthday, so we about to chill. You should slide through."

"I told you clubbing is not my thing. I'll be here waiting for you to get home. I love you, Prada."

"I love you too, ma."

Gavin leaned down, and we engaged in a passionate kiss. Before I could even attempt to try to drop this dick off in her, she hopped out of bed. After facing the blunt and contemplating, I knew what I had to do. There was no need for me to prolong the shit anymore.

Jumping from the bed, I rushed inside the bathroom but stopped in my tracks. Gavin was popping a birth control pill. To witness that fucked me up in the head. I quickly hid the box in my hand behind my back. I was about to ask her to marry me but changed my mind. We discussed having a baby when I came home. She acted as if she was on board about taking that step. Seeing this lets me know that she's not.

"Let me explain!"

"Nah, you good! Don't wait up."

I threw the ring box in the garbage and quickly got the fuck out of dodge. It had fucked me up feeling like she wasn't ready for what I was ready for. Honestly, this was the first time in my adult life I wanted to do right by a female.

7

GAVIN

My heart felt like it had cracked in half. The last thing I wanted was Prada to catch me taking birth control pills. We had agreed that we would try for a baby. He expressed how he was ready to be a father, and I was on board. However, neither of us was really ready. He had just got out of jail and there was no guarantee on the future of his freedom. That added with all the businesses we have to run. Right now wasn't a good time to have a baby. I feel bad because I should have expressed this to him. Knowing Prada, he's probably overthinking who I am as a person. Lord knows I want to be with him and him only. After all, he has been there for me in ways I could never have imagined. Finding the ring in the wastebasket hurt my heart. It was as if he was saying fuck our future and I couldn't let that shit ride.

"Your ass is not about to be riding with me all in your feelings." Ms. Gladys was driving me crazy. She had me high and drinking some damn Crown Royal.

"I'm sorry, Ms. Gladys. Prada is so mad at me. Just tell me what to do so I can make it up to him." My ass was desperate at this point. Prada wasn't answering my calls or anything, and the shit had me on the verge of tears.

"If you want to make it with Prada, you have to handle him differently. He needs to be nurtured and coddled. Now, I'm not saying don't make him be the man he needs to be. What I'm saying is love on him extra cause he needs it. You see, Prada, that's my baby right there. He suffers from middle child syndrome. People always love on the oldest and the youngest kids, and the middle child sometimes gets lost in the shuffle. Prada has always had issues. Like, he pops off, and once he's pissed, it's hard to calm him down. It's your job to learn his triggers. This ain't that shit with Carlo. You're fucking with a real thoroughbred ass nigga. He can have a heart of gold and a heart of ice at the same time. Stop worrying. He's just in his feelings. Trust me. That boy is crazy about you. I thought he was losing his mind when he asked for the ring his mother left for him and his brothers."

"That's his mother's ring."

"Yeah. Before she died, she purchased each of them rings to give to their wives when they decide to take that leap. My daughter had her shit together for them boys' future. She just didn't anticipate being murdered while I was doing time. Don't worry, Gavin. Prada Alexander vowed to never marry a bitch or have kids. He wants those things with you. Now perk the fuck up and grab your gun."

Ms. Gladys parked the car, and we jumped out. This lady had a damn light switch in her brain. She could literally change within the blink of an eye.

"What are we doing over here?" We were at Smitty's lounge. This was the nigga who owed Prada money and was refusing to pay me when I came to collect.

"Don't this nigga owe you money? I hear he's been dodging you. Let me show you how to get your shit."

"If ain't Gladys Alexander! To what do I owe this gracious presence?"

"Smitty, this is not a social call. Run me my mother-fucking money. That is not a request, nigga!" Ms. Gladys took her Glock out and set it on the corner.

"Hold on now. I told her I would give it to her when I got it. Pulling out your gun in my establishment is not cause for."

"You playing with my nigga's money is what wasn't caused for was." I upped my gun on his ass because clearly he thought I was a joke.

"Shoot that nigga, baby!"

The sound of Prada's voice made my heart race. *What the hell was he doing here?* Looking over at Ms. Gladys, I peeped her sly grin. She knew his ass was coming out here.

"Come on now, P! I got your money right here. I'll even add five thousand more for your troubles." Smitty was begging and pleading for his life. The whole time Ms. Gladys was laughing at his ass.

The feeling of Prada standing directly behind me made the hairs on the back of my neck stand up.

"Shoot that nigga right now! That way, he knows when you come back to collect, you're not playing with his ass." Prada gritted in my ear.

His words were like the boost I needed it. Without further hesitation, I pulled the trigger hitting him in the shoulder.

"Ahhhhhhhh!"

"That a girl. Grab the money and let's get the hell out of here. I'll see you on the first, Smitty!" Prada yelled over his shoulder as we all walked out of the lounge. Smitty ass was still on the floor writhing around in pain and crying.

"You nice with that trigger finger. Lose the hesitation,

and we're good to go," Ms. Gladys said as she winked her eye at me. Prada was walking ahead of us like it was nothing.

"Let me talk to you for a minute, Prada!" I yelled.

"We'll talk later. Get on out of here." Prada jumped in his car and peeled off. I prayed he got over being mad at me sooner or later. This bipolar behavior was about to get on my fucking nerves.

NIGHTTIME HAD FALLEN, and Prada still hadn't answered or called me. At this hour, I knew that Nettie's party was in full swing. I stood in the floor-length mirror of our bedroom with nothing on but my Team Supreme chain. The diamonds in the money sign glistened as I moved my neck from side to side. I couldn't believe that I was a part of something so prestigious. Yeah, I know it's a criminal enterprise, but the rush is something that makes me look over that. I've never felt this way before. As a matter of fact, this may be the first time I'm able to express my feelings.

With my parents and Carlo, I suppressed my feelings in an effort to keep the peace. I feel like being a part of Team Supreme requires me to make a level of noise to demand my respect from Prada. I'm not some bitch he rescued that he can handle any type of way.

Granted he has every right to be mad at me. However, ignoring me will not be tolerated. For years, I fought for my voice to be heard being married to Carlo. I don't want life to be that way with Prada. It's imperative I demand my respect expeditiously.

Clubbing is not my thing, but tonight I'll have to make an exception. Waiting for him to come home and talk was not going to cut it. Gavin Mills waits for no one anymore, not even the sexy, rich, and handsome Prada Alexander.

"BITCH, the drug dealers are out tonight! I'm glad you called me to ride shotgun."

"I advise you to put them hormones away. Bitch, I will not help your ass fight Fendi's crazy ass."

"Bitch, you better square up right beside me. Don't forget that time I put Carlo's car on a flat and put Snickers in his gas tank!"

I fell out laughing because he was pissed off. I swear Miyani and Dream were always doing shit to fuck with Carlo. It used to take everything inside of me to keep from laughing.

"Yeah, you got me. I owe you big time, sis."

"Now, listen, we walk in this bitch, and we going to keep it real player. No matter how Prada acts, do not cut on his ass. Don't ever argue with your nigga in front of these hoes. Do that shit in the privacy of your home. What bitches don't know about your personal business, they can't speak on. Now let's get us a drink because I need to be tipsy for this shit."

I took a deep breath and proceeded into the club. Immediately, my nerves sat in. The club was so crowded with people. My ass has always been afraid of crowds, so this was fucking with my anxiety.

"What's good, Dream? What can I get y'all?" the bartender asked as she wiped down the counter.

"Have a setup of Rémy sent up to section eight?"

"Why are you in a section? The whole team is partying up on the top floor."

"We're just here to check out the scene," Dream said, and we headed up the spiral staircase. Big ass screens surrounded the club. You could actually see what was going on in the other sections and the dancefloors.

"This place is nice. Dream, you did all of this?" I looked around in amazement at the interior. When the guys got locked up, Dream single handedly turned around all of Fendi's businesses.

"Girl, yes, I'm so glad Fendi's ass is out so that I no longer have to deal with these trifling ass bitches. I fired so many hoes when I get here. They were stealing time, doing drugs with the customers, and overall doing whatever they fuck they want to do. These new girls are much classier."

The bottle girl came over and placed our bottles at the table. I quickly took the shot from her hand as she poured it. My ass needed to relax.

"I don't think I could be around these naked ass women all day." Just thinking about it had me in my feelings. Prada's ass swore he needed to come up here for business. Now that I see what that business was, I'm going to kill his ass.

"I'm still not used to it, especially, with Fendi being out and back working the day-to-day operations. At the same time, I'm so secure in my relationship with Fendi these days. This is the first time I've experienced a love this real. Can't no hoe fuck that up."

As I sat and thought about it, I agreed with Dream. This love with Prada is different, and I love everything about it. His touch alone makes me feel so safe and secure. Fuck sitting here and drinking. I needed to go upstairs to him.

"I'll be back, sis. I'm about to go up here and talk to Prada."

"You want me to go with you in case that nigga jump stupid?"

"Nah, Dream, sit ya ass right there and until I come back." I laughed at her crazy ass as I knocked back my shot.

Quickly walking off, I headed up to the top floor where they were. As soon as I locked eyes with him, his mouth started to twitch. I could tell he was angry. Most likely because of the short ass dress I was wearing.

"What's good, Sis? Where's Dream stanking ass at?"

"Hey, Fendi, she's downstairs in section eight chilling." He quickly jumped up and headed out of the section. I prayed they asses didn't get to arguing. That's all they do is fight and fuck and then do the shit all over again.

"I thought clubbing wasn't your thing?" Prada asked while looking straight ahead. The nigga wouldn't even look at me and talk.

"It's not, Prada."

"Then what are you doing here. You damn near naked in this bitch. As you can look around, I'm sure you see how you fit in." He turned up the Hennessy bottle and drank straight from it. It was truly a fucking trigger seeing him doing that and talking fucked up to me.

"Aye, P! Not cool lil bro!" G said as he walked over to Prada.

"Fall back, gangsta! Save all that energy for her sister. Now like I asked what the fuck are you doing here?" he yelled so damn loud he got damn near everyone's attention. Embarrassed was an understatement.

"I advise you to stop yelling at me. As a matter of fact, let's go home. You've had enough to drink! I walked over to him and snatched the bottle from his hand.

"What the fuck are you doing? Last time I checked, my mother was dead. Who the fuck are you to tell me I've had enough?"

At this point, I was over this shit and fed the fuck up. If

it's one thing I hate, it's a drunk, belligerent, dumb ass nigga. Right now, I was more embarrassed for him than I was for me. He's something big in these streets. He's a part of Team Supreme, so respect is a must off the rip. These niggas would love to see him out here bad. I could never let him go out like that.

"I'm your woman, and I said you've had enough. Cut the bullshit, Prada Alexander! Tell ya crew goodnight, my nigga!"

I forcefully grabbed his ass and led him out of the section. The whole team was laughing at his ass. As we headed down the stairs, Fendi and Dream were walking up hand in hand.

"Where y'all going?"

"Home, this nigga is fucked up, and it's a wrap. I'll see you at Sunday dinner tomorrow."

"Oh shit! You got to go night-night, nigga!" Fendi teased Prada.

"Man, babe, why you had to come and do me like that in front of the crew? Now I'm going to have to shoot one of them niggas."

"Shut up, Prada!" I continued to pull him out of the section and down the stairs. People were still coming up the stairs.

The moment I clinched Prada's hand tighter, a masked gunman stepped directly in front of us and started shooting. It was as if Prada was no longer drunk. That nigga knocked me to the floor and got on top of me so fast. All I could do was cover my ears as gunshots rang out around me. Then just like that, it stopped.

"You okay, baby?" Prada yanked me up from the floor and started searching my body frantically. I was doing the same to him. My damn heart was racing so bad. Looking around the club, I saw a couple of people laid out. One that I did take notice of was the gunman who started shooting at us.

"I'm fine."

I grabbed his face and kissed him deeply. My ass was no longer mad at his ass. All of that shit went out the window the moment they got to shooting. This was definitely my last time at a fucking club.

"Butta! Get Gavin and Dream out of here. As a matter of fact, all of y'all head home. I'll clean this shit up and talk to the police." G was pissed as he walked back and forth trying to calm down. The nigga had morphed from a gentleman to a gangster real quick. The nigga was also toting a gun bigger than my damn body. I pray my sister don't make him mad because his ass goes from zero to one hundred.

"Nah, G, we can't leave you, bro!" Prada stated.

"We all own this bitch, so Prada and I will stay with you! Butta, get my baby home safe." Fendi grabbed Dream and kissed her. Even in the midst of everything going on, he was still concerned about her. They were so cute with their bi-polar asses.

"I'll be home later." Prada walked past me and stomped the shit out of the nigga that shot at us.

"Bitch ass nigga!" Seeing him so angry made me hurry up and follow Butta out of the club. While I know he has a mean streak, I love the softer side of him.

"You okay, sis?" Dream asked.

"Yeah, I'm good. I just can't wait to get home to my son."

For the rest of the ride, we were all silent like we hadn't just been in a damn shootout. I couldn't wait to get home and call Miyani.

8

MIYANI

My eyes instantly shot open hearing the shower running. It was well after four in the morning, and G was just getting home. Gavin had already hit me up and let me know about what kicked off at the club. I had been a nervous wreck all night. After trying my best to wait up, I ended up falling asleep. This mother of two thing has me tired as fuck. It's been three weeks since I gave birth, and I still feel like I was hit by a truck.

Hearing the water stop running, I sat up in bed. G stepped out of the bedroom minutes later with a towel wrapped around his waist.

"I'm sorry, beautiful. Did I wake you up?" He walked over to the bed and kissed me on the forehead.

"No, you didn't wake me up. I was actually waiting for you to come home. Is everybody okay?"

Damn, I wish my six weeks was up. Givenchy dropped his towel and placed on a pair of Ethika underwear. My baby dick was so long and thick. I was salivating just thinking about the feeling of it.

"Team Supreme is always good. Let's get some sleep

before the kids get up. It's Sunday, and you know my grandma will be calling bright and early telling us to be on time for dinner." G climbed in bed and kissed me once more on the lips before lying down.

Not wanting to press the issue, I laid my head on his chest. All day I anticipated him coming home so that I could do this very thing. He felt so safe and secure. On the other hand, I couldn't help but wonder if we really were safe and secure. This man was just in a shootout that left several bodies back at the club, yet here he was lightly snoring as if nothing had happened.

THE NEXT AFTERNOON G was still sleeping, and I refused to wake him up. This was probably the best sleep he has had since he's been out. Hearing my son cry over the monitor made me quickly rushed into the nursery. He was screaming at the top of his lungs with his spoiled ass. Lord have mercy, this son of mine was going to have to stop this crying. It was driving me crazy. It was my own fault, though.

From the moment I gave birth, I've held my son nonstop, picking him up when he cries and letting him sleep on my chest. It seems like I just laid him down and here he wanted to be picked up. It's like he knows when he's not with me

"Shhh! Stop crying before you wake up daddy."

"Too late. The lil nigga already woke me up."

Looking up from G-Baby, I observed G fully dressed and headed out. My ass became disappointed quick. He had been gone so much, and I hadn't been able to get a moment of his time. Givenchy spoiled me rotten before he got locked up. That man always spent time with me, and now, it's like he has no time at all.

"You're leaving already? It seems like you just came home." G came over and took G-Baby from my hand.

"Hey, son! What's good, my prince? Daddy loves you."

I smiled looking at G love all over our son. The way he talks to him is so cute. No matter how much G-Baby is crying, he stops as soon as G starts talking to him.

"I ordered some seafood. You want to eat lunch with me before you head out." I grabbed him by the bottom of his shirt and pulled him close. After engaging in a passionate kiss, he handed G-Baby back to me.

"Nah, I'm going to save my appetite for Sunday dinner at my grandma's. I'll meet y'all over there. I need to handle some shit at the warehouse. Don't trip. I promise to spend the rest day with you and the kids. How many more weeks you have before we can fuck?"

"About three?"

"That shit needs to hurry up. A nigga needs some pussy. I love you, beautiful."

"I love you too. Please be careful, Givenchy." We exchanged a deep kiss and a hug before he headed out.

Sitting down in the rocking chair, I contemplated on if I really wanted to go over to Ms. Gladys' house for dinner. I would much rather stay at home. However, she wouldn't dare let me miss Sunday dinner with the family.

Once I put my son to sleep, I decided to check some emails. My heart immediately began to race looking at the wire transfer I had sent a realtor. Apparently, someone gave them a better offer on the space. My ass had been looking for a bigger dance studio in a better location. This space was perfect. Once I secured the space and signed the papers, I thought everything was done. This is absolutely crazy. I didn't give a fuck that it was a Sunday. That realtor was about to get cussed the fuck out. The bitch cannot take the money, have me sign the paperwork, and then send the fucking money back. This bitch was going to tell me what the fuck was going on. This shit here was unprofessional as hell. Quickly I got G-Baby and I dressed. I didn't have time to find a sitter or call G. This shit needed to be handled now.

"WHERE IS DEANNE? I wasted no time getting straight to it when I walked inside of her agency. This half-breed ass bitch had me so fucked up.

"I'm sorry. She's not seeing anyone right now."

"She'll make an exception for me." Without hesitation, I pushed my stroller right past her ass.

"Heyy! You can't go in there." She jumped up and tried to grab me, but I was too quick for her. The moment I walked inside of her office, I knew who was behind me losing my space — my mother, Melissa Mills.

"It's okay, Hannah." DeAnne quickly stood and damn near pushed her receptionist out of the office.

"I guess I know why I received my money back."

"Have a seat, Miyani. All the theatrics aren't necessary. Excuse us for a minute, DeAnne. I need to talk to my daughter." The last thing I wanted to do was talk to this evil ass woman.

"Of course, Mrs. Mills." This silly broad damn near ran out of her own office. My baby started to whine, so I quickly tended to him.

"Let me see my grandson. It's a shame you have kept him from your parents. Do you hate us that much?"

"I don't hate anyone. At the same time, why shouldn't I hate you? You've mistreated me damn near all of my life. It took for me to get in a real relationship to see just how evil you are. What type of mother blocks her own daughters from their happiness? You being here answers my question as to who outbid me on that space. Why would you do that?"

I hated that I was getting emotional. There I was sitting in tears in front of the one woman I should never let see me cry. She loved this shit. The look on her face showed how happy she was about the pain I was in. My son started to squirm and cry in her arms. He knew the bitch was evil. I quickly grabbed him from her ass.

"Why must everything be so theatrical with you? I have been the best mother that I could be to you and Gavin. Nothing is ever good enough for you. Your father and I spoiled you and didn't get you ready for the real world. Now that you think you're a part of this family that you think holds all the power."

Before I could respond to her, she reached over and snatched my Team Supreme chain from around my neck. My reflexes made me slap the fuck out of her. Her lip started to bleed instantly.

"Don't ever put your fucking hands on me again."

"You're dead to me, Miyani Mills. Say goodbye to your precious dance studio. I plan on taking everything you love, including my grandson. Trust me. There is nothing that motherfucker Givenchy Alexander can do. I curse the day that you were born. Tell your sister she's dead to me as well. Now, if you don't mind, I would like to finish this business deal, and you're trespassing."

I wanted to beat this lady ass so badly, but I had my baby. He was crying at the top of his lungs, and I had to get out of there. Upset was an understatement for the way I was feeling. My mother and I could never come back from this moment.

"My son is the only reason I'm not tap dancing on your head, you evil, spiteful, conniving ass bitch. Melissa Mills, you have been dead to me. Givenchy will murder your ass behind us. Tread lightly with your threats. They don't move me at all. I feel sorry for my father. You have ruined that man's relationship with his daughters."

"Newsflash! He's not your father, bitch! Your father is common gutta trash just like your ass. Now, he's definitely Gavin's father. The only reason Gavin and my relationship is over is because of you. Your jealous manipulative ass got in her head and made her fuck her life up.

"Is everything okay, Ms. Mills?"

"Everything is fine. My daughter was just leaving. Let's finish this deal." She grinned at me and sat back in the chair she was previously sitting in.

A part of me stood there is shock at her revelation. I stared at her looking for something that would tell me she was speaking out of anger. Unfortunately, I didn't see what I was hoping for. All I saw was the truth — Malcolm Mills wasn't my father.

I had so many questions, but I knew that she wasn't about to tell me anything. She had won this round. Unfortunately, I was crushed. My heart was aching to the part where it was hurting. I was shaking like a leaf as I placed my son back in his car seat. After putting the stroller away in the trunk, I quickly got the fuck from there.

The whole ride home I cried out of hurt and confusion. Why would she say that to me like that? Maybe that's why she hates me? I'm not his, but I have his last name. What the fuck was going on right now? I was so upset that I ended up going back home instead of Ms. Gladys' house for Sunday dinner.

I was so in shock that I couldn't think straight. Instead of bothering G, I laid my son down and tried to wrap my mind around this bullshit. All I could do was cry as I laid across my bed. Although I was grown as fuck, I felt like a lost little girl. The man I've loved all my life is not my father, and that shit hurts. It was crazy how that revelation made me realize just how different from them I was. Now I could see how much Gavin looked like him, and I had nothing of him. I looked like her and that made me hurt more. She was officially dead to me. *What did I do to deserve this life?* I thought to myself as I drifted off to sleep.

～

"MIYANI, WAKE UP!" the sound of G's booming voice made me quickly sit up.

Once I was able to focus, I observed him walking back and forth trying to calm down the baby. Of course, his crybaby ass was yelling at the top of his lungs.

"Oh shit! I fell asleep. Mommy is so sorry." I grabbed him and placed a kiss on his forehead. He looked like he had been crying for a long period of time.

"Miyani, we were worried about you. Why didn't you come to Sunday dinner? Grandma Gladys is pissed off," Gianna said.

"Language, Gianna."

"I'm sorry, daddy. Let me hold him. I can make him stop crying." She jumped up on the couch, and I handed G-Baby to her. Gianna was the biggest help I had with the baby. She knew how to hold him properly, feed, and then burp him, not to mention put him to sleep.

Rushing into the kitchen, I grabbed him a bottle and quickly tried to warm it up as much as I could.

"Talk to me, Miyani! Why the fuck didn't you answer the

phone for me? You had me thinking you were coming to Sunday dinner and didn't show up. Since when do you fall asleep on him like that? Thank God, I made it here on time. The cover was on his face while he screamed and cried. That shit is not cool. If you need a nanny so that you can rest we can hire one! He could have died, Miyani!"

I was trying my best to hold in my tears. G was yelling out of frustration. After the day I had, the last thing I needed was him in getting down on me.

"I know, Givenchy. Please stop yelling. I'm sorry I fell asleep." I quickly walked away from him and handed Gianna the bottle. The tears were welling up in my eyes, and the last thing I wanted was for him to see me crying.

"I'll be back, Gianna. Call me if you need me, okay."

"Miyani!" G yelled my name, but I continued to walk up the stairs.

Right now, I couldn't deal with him judging my parenting, even though I know he's right. G-Baby could have died. I could never forgive myself if that had happened. Taking notice of my chain she ripped from my neck overwhelmed me. The tears freely flowed as I sat on the edge of the bed. I could feel G's presence in the room, but I refused to look up. It's something about being vulnerable in front of such a strong man. I'm supposed to be stronger than this. I'm supposed to be stronger for him.

"I'm only going to ask you one time, Miyani. What the fuck is wrong with you? When I left this afternoon, you were fine. I come home to you sleeping, and G-Baby was screaming at the top of his lungs. Now you're sitting here crying your ass off. Hold up! What the fuck happened to your chain, Miyani?"

"My mother snatched it off." Tears dropped, and I quickly wiped my face.

"What the fuck you mean she snatched it off?" G rushed over from where he was standing and stood over me.

"I told you that I had secured the space and paid for it. When you left, I checked my email, and DeAnne had sent the money back to the account. I was furious because I knew it was some bullshit. I knew you needed to handle something, and I didn't have time to call someone to keep him for me. Without hesitation, I rushed to her office. When I made it there, my mother was sitting in her office. Right then and there I knew she was behind it. Of course, she had to start with her evilness, threatening us and shit. Before I knew it, she snatched my chain from my neck. That's when I slapped her ass. I guess that really angered her because she revealed to me that Malcolm Mills isn't really my father.

I thought she was just trying to hurt me, but she was serious, babe. Why did she even give birth to me? What did I do that was so bad to make her treat me this way?"

I was so damn embarrassed crying ugly as hell like this. Snot was running all out of my nose. G pulled me up from where I was sitting and cradled me like a baby. This man that I'm madly in love with literally rocked me back and forth until I stopped crying. He didn't speak a word. He just allowed me to get my emotions out of the way. I had my face snuggled in the nape of his neck, inhaling his Sauvage cologne. That mixed with the sound of his powerful heartbeat made me feel better.

"I want you to get all of that shit out of your system now. You can cry, scream, and break something if you have to. After that, there will be no more crying over that bitch. Any tears after today is unacceptable in my eyes. Miyani Alexander, you're far too good for the evils of this world. Your mother is an evil and wicked ass person. She doesn't deserve to have such a beautiful soul as a daughter. Miyani, I'm going to murder your mother. As your nigga, I will never sit back and allow anyone to mistreat you. This shit has been going on for so long, and it has to be ended. Your mother is like a cancer that won't stop growing. In order for us to live a good life comfortably, we have to get rid of the cancer. Do you understand what I'm saying, Miyani?" G spoke softly but sternly.

"Yes, Givenchy, I hear you loud and clear."

"Good. Now you've had a long day. I'll get the kids ready for bed, and we can chill for the rest of the night." G kissed me and headed out of our bedroom. I don't know what the fuck I did to deserve a man like Givenchy Alexander. Whatever it was, I'm glad I did it.

Since G was tending to the kids, I decided to take me a long hot bath. While bathing, all I could think about was Gavin. How was I supposed to tell her what our mother revealed to me? All of our lives we've been raised to believe that we shared the same mother and father. The more I thought about the shit, the more I knew I had to investigate my mother. Something was off, and I had to get down to the bottom of it. Once I gathered all the information, I would reveal everything to my sister. In the meantime, Dream was going to help me. She's good at this type of shit. Plus, it's right up her alley to fuck with my mother.

"So, let me get this straight. That old bitch just revealed it to you like that?"

"Yes! She didn't have a care in the world. I wish you could have been there. It was nothing to her. I can't get her facial expression out of my head. She wanted to hurt me."

Dream and I were sitting on the patio of her house sipping wine and talking.

"I wish I had been there with you. It would have taken the jaws of life to get my hands from around her scrawny ass neck. Have you talked to your father about this?"

"No! I don't even know if I could face him. My ass hasn't revealed this shit to Gavin either. I want to find out some shit on my mother. That's where you come in at. You have to help me do some investigating."

"Bitch, you already know I'm down for that. I already never liked her old ass. That stunt she pulled behind that police hoe made me hate her ass. She spoke so highly of her while talking down to you. That shit hurt my heart, Miyani. Like, you're so good of a person. What the fuck could you have possibly done to make her treat you so bad? I'm here for you no matter what. I'll always have your back just like you've always had mine."

"Aww, bitch, don't make me cry!"

"Wipe your damn face. The only one going to be crying around this bitch is your ugly ass mammy. She done tried you for the last time."

We toasted to that and took a sip of wine. Knowing that I had Dream on board to help made me feel so much better. Melissa Mills had officially fucked with me for the last time.

9

GIVENCHY

Seeing my baby cry angered the fuck out of me. Miyani is like the sweetest person in the world. It fucks me up to know that her mother treats her the way that she does. That's one of the main reasons I go overboard when it comes to her. She deserves to be praised and complimented every moment of the day.

Miyani deserves to be spoiled and treated with respect. She doesn't go out of her way to hurt people. Miyani has the purest soul and a heart of gold. She definitely deserves better than what her mother is doing to her. Now, I understand why the fuck she's so mean to her. The loose pussy bitch has been living a lie. I'm sure it's more to this shit than that. I plan to get down to the bottom of all this shit. Her old ass will not keep hurting Miyani.

It was so much going on around me that I couldn't think straight. This shit with Miyani's mother only added more to the bullshit that I had on my plate. In the midst of dealing with this street shit, I felt like I had been lacking with Miyani. She had given birth to my son and accepted my daughter as her own. Plus, she's been running my shit like a boss. She had finally gotten the city to accept the fact that The Chanel House and Supreme Suites were good ideas. They were no longer fighting us on it, and they would be opening within the next two months. Miyani had surprised me in so many ways. I took notice of how she tried to always be perfect for me. That didn't sit well because I wanted Miyani to be free. I could only imagine how hard her childhood was trying to live up to her mother's standards.

Miyani had no clue that I was the one who needed to live up to her standards. She was the perfect woman for a nigga like me. I just had to work ten times harder not to fuck shit up. Team Supreme has always been my first priority outside of Gianna, but now that I have Miyani and our son. My priorities have changed. The family I created first and Team Supreme second.

"I NEED to call and check on the baby."

"No. He's fine, Miyani. My grandma's got him covered. Just relax." From the moment we left the house, she had been worried about the baby.

"This is my first time since giving birth that I've been away from him. I miss him." I reached across the table and took her damn phone. She needed to enjoy herself. A nigga had pulled out all the stops to treat her to a nice night on the town.

"I know, baby, but tonight it's all about you. You know my granny is gone make sure he's straight."

"That doesn't make me feel better. The last time we were at her house, she threatened to put beer in his damn bottle if he didn't stop crying." I tried my best not to laugh because she would definitely do it.

"She raised my brothers and me. Look at us. We all turned out fine."

"You are perfect. Now your crazy brothers I don't know about. It's obvious she put too much damn beer in their bottles."

Before I could say anything, the sound of someone clearing their throat caught my attention. Looking up, it was some unknown nigga standing over us. I quickly gripped my pistol that sat on my lap underneath the table.

"What's good, Miyani?"

"Ain't shit good, my nigga! Who the fuck is you?" I placed my gun on the table to let him know I wasn't about to play with his ass. He looked like a square ass nigga from the looks of his eyes. The nigga was shook at the sight of my gun.

"Get away from this table, Noonie. You and I both know we have nothing to say to each other."

"Pump ya brakes! I come in peace. I just wanted to speak. That's all."

"Don't speak to my wife! As a matter of fact, get the fuck away from this table before I shoot you!" The nigga put his hands up in defeat and walked off. I smirked at his coward ass.

"Who the fuck is that nigga, and why was he saying your name?"

Yeah, I was feeling a little jealous. Miyani was mine, and I didn't want a nigga around her at all. Him having the balls to step to her didn't sit well with me. It felt personal to me.

"That's my ex-boyfriend, Noonie. We have been broken up for damn near two years. We were together during high school, and I basically helped his ass through college in an effort to keep his football scholarship. When he went pro, he left me. That same week, I found out he was getting married and had a baby on the way. It took me some time to get over that. For a long time, I didn't want to be in a relationship. You're the first man I've been with since the relationship with him ended. Now put your gun away because he ain't worth a bullet. I'm here with you, and all I want is you." Miyani reached across the table and kissed me on the lips.

"I'm sorry I blew up like that."

"Oh no, don't be sorry. It turns me on to have a man that doesn't play behind me. I've never felt so safe and secure. Plus, it's kind of cute seeing you all jealous."

"That nigga almost lost his life by simply saying your name." I knocked back my shot as my phone started to go off. I quickly pressed ignore. It was India begging for a weekend visit with Gianna.

"Who was that?"

"That was India. She wants Gianna for the weekend. I'm just not feeling it at all. All of a sudden, she shows up wanting to be a mother. How am I supposed to subject my daughter to some shit like that? Now she's talking about she's back to stay for good and wants to be in Gianna's life. I'm just not with the shit at all."

India was getting on my nerves, consistently calling for my daughter. I didn't give a fuck that she came out of her pussy. The bitch was not her mother. The hoe was a deadbeat. India wasn't fooling me though. She was trying to come back and stir some shit up. She hated that I was in a relationship with Miyani. She's doing nothing but using Gianna as a pawn in her sick ass game. I can't even kill her because there is no telling what the fuck she's mixed up in.

"I don't trust her period. That bitch followed me all around when you were locked up. We really need to go speak to an attorney or come up with some type of plan. Gianna is mixed up in something she had no idea about.

With India, you never know. Givenchy, you need to make sure we have all of our shit together. Gianna would be devastated if India pulled some shit and had her removed from our home. I couldn't handle that."

"You don't have anything to worry about. I've already talked with the courts. I'm her primary guardian and India is the one that needs to prove herself to the court system. Thanks for loving my daughter the way that you do. She's never experienced that type of love. It's like you went from simply being her ballet teacher to be the mother that she never had. Now you've given me the son I've always wanted. A nigga couldn't ask for a better woman in my life. You're the realest on my team Miyani! Come on. Let's get out of here. I have something I need to show you."

I knew that being with Miyani is the best decision I've ever made. She loved everything about me and everything that I loved. Marriage has never been on my radar. With her, she makes me want to officially give her my last name. From the moment I met her, I knew she would be my wife one day. I just needed to let this shit play out and see where it went. It's safe to say it went exactly the way I wanted it to.

One Hour Later

"What are we doing here, Givenchy?"

"From the moment we met, you always expressed to me your love for dancing. Seeing how dedicated you were to creating young black beautiful ballerinas moved me. When I enrolled Gianna, I would come early just to see you dance. I know that Tippy Toes Dance Studio is everything to you. There was no way I could sit back and let your mother just take the space from you. Here these are yours."

I dropped the keys to the new Tippy Toes Dance Studio in her hand.

"Oh my god! How did you do this? DeAnne sent me the money back."

"Let's just say I gave DeAnne an offer she didn't refuse."

"Thank you so much, Givenchy! I can't believe this. The girls are going to be so happy about all the extra space."

Miyani was walking all around, just taking in the massive ass space. I couldn't wait for her to decorate it. She had handled all of my business while I was away, so it was imperative she focused on her dance studio. Waiting for the right moment, I got down on one knee. Hell, it was the perfect time to pop the question. Seconds later, she turned around and immediately covered her mouth.

"Oh my god, Givenchy!"

"Come on now. Stop that crying. This isn't a sad occasion. It's obvious I'm fucked up about ya beautiful ass. From the moment I walked into your dance studio, I knew that I wanted something with you. At that time, I didn't know what that was so I decided to throw caution to the wind. Here we are a year later, and shit is better than I ever expected. You carried my seed , you rocking my chain, and all that's needed is for you to carry my last name. So, what's it going to be beautiful?"

"Yes, Givenchy Alexander, I will be honored to carry your last name."

"I know that it's traditional for niggas to buy huge engagement rings, but this ring is extremely special to me. Before my mother left this world, she left my brothers and me these rings. They were meant for the woman we chose to spend the rest of our lives with. There isn't another woman out here worthy enough to wear it. Placing this ring on your finger means we're locked in for life."

"It would make me more than happy to wear your mother's ring. I love you more than life itself. Hurry up and put the damn ring on my finger before I change my mind."

As I placed the ring on her finger, we engaged in a passionate kiss. We stood in the middle of the empty dance studio loving on each other. I couldn't believe I was about to be someone's husband. At the same time, I'm ready for the challenge. Now that I have this damn proposal out of the way, I can handle this street shit accordingly.

"So, when the fuck were you going to tell us about dealing with Slim?" I asked Fendi. His ass owed us an explanation about the shit.

That nigga may have murdered our mother, so fucking with him on the low got me questioning his motives, which is something I've never had to question. Bro has always been loyal to a fault. This shit is so out of his character. That's why it's mindboggling that he would keep this shit to himself.

"Yeah, bro, you doing business with that nigga and didn't tell granny. She is gone fuck you up when she finds out."

"I'm a grown ass man dawg. I don't have to explain shit to anyone in regard to my decisions. You niggas raised me, so trust, anything I do, it's for a reason, not to mention for the greater good of Team Supreme. Silk reached out to me when he got out of prison. At first, I didn't fuck with him on any level. I even threatened to murk his ass if he tried to reach out to me. He knew neither of you would fuck with him. It wasn't until he told me he had proof of who killed mommy. I'm sorry I didn't tell you all sooner. As far as me doing business with him, we've never done business. He doesn't know shit about our operation. What the fuck you take me for some weak ass nigga? You think I'm walking around with Team Supreme branded on my back for nothing. Don't ever question my loyalty! This shit is til the death of me!"

"Respect bro, however, you should have told us something. Imagine how I felt hearing that bitch India tell me that shit.

"Wait a minute. How does that bitch know anything?"

"Really, Prada? She's a police ass bitch. That's how the fuck she knows. I'm telling y'all something ain't right about this bitch popping up like this. We have to get rid of her ass." Fendi was hype as fuck as he knocked back a shot.

"Nobody wants to get rid of the bitch more than I do. We can't make a hasty decision that we will regret later. She claims to be done with working for the FEDS. I'm still baffled behind the hoe saying she's ready to be a mother. I've been avoiding the bitch like the plague. I know she's up to no good. I'm trying to protect Miyani, G-Baby, and most importantly, Gianna. India doesn't mean her any fucking good."

I took a long pull from the blunt I was smoking. It was the only thing that could calm down at the moment. The thought of the bitch angered me to the point where I wanted to punch something.

"Speak of the devil, and they will appear. Look who's outside?" Gunna said. We all turned our heads towards the computer screen, and it was the bitch India.

"This is why I say the hoe got to go. What would make her think popping up here at headquarters was cool? Let me murk that hoe, big bro." Prada had pulled his gun out and headed towards the entrance.

"Put the gun away, Prada. It's better to keep our enemies close. What better way than for us to know her motives?"

I hit the button that manually opened up the doors. We were all sitting around the conference table waiting for the rat ass hoe to appear.

"I see not much has changed. This takes me back to the good times."

"What the fuck you want, rat?"

"Calm down, killa! I come in peace."

"Peace these nuts, hoe! Now, what the fuck you want?" Prada jumped up from where he was sitting, and I quickly caught him before he lunged at her.

"I see them Percs still have your ass going crazy."

"I'm good, bro. I got something for your ass. Just be easy."

"Look, I didn't come here to fight with y'all. What's done is done. I can't take the shit back. At the same time, it's because of me that none of you are in jail serving life behind bars. Instead of talking shit to me, you should be thanking me. I'm not even here for all of that. A bitch is only stepping foot in here for the sake of my daughter. All Givenchy had to do was answer my calls."

"I didn't have to do shit. India, get the fuck out of here. I already told your ass what the fuck is. Talk to my attorney."

"She's not her daughter, G! No matter what has happened. Nothing will change the fact that I gave birth to Gianna Versace Alexander! That's my daughter, G. I want to see her. Please let me at least tell her my side."

"Your side is irrelevant. Get the fuck out of my place of business! This is a rat-free zone. I'll see you at the custody hearing and not a moment sooner."

"That bitch got you all fucked up in the head!"

"You're absolutely right! I'm so gone over my baby that I put a ring on it, bitch!"

The life drained out of India's face hearing that. I knew it would. She was working with them police, but she was fucked up by a nigga.

"I guess I'll see you and that bitch in court! She may have my life, but she'll never have my daughter. Tread lightly with me, G. It's better to be my friend and not my enemy." She quickly walked off and out of the office. I couldn't wait for this court case to be over so that I can murk her ass.

10

———

GLADYS ALEXANDER

Usually, I don't do too much motherfucking talking. I say what I mean, and I mean what the fuck I say. Retirement has been all good, but I'm back on my OG shit. Apparently, motherfuckers forget who really runs this shit. I'm not a praying woman like I should be. However, when my grandsons were locked up, I prayed that they would beat the shit.

It was the first time I wasn't sure that they would beat the case.

When I walked inside of the courtroom and saw Joseph, I knew God had heard my prayers. I'm still processing the fact that we have been reunited. After all of these years nothing had changed. The motherfucker was still a crook. To make matters worse he held people freedom in his hands.

I've been waiting for my stubborn ass grandkids to come around. It's been a minute since they've been out, and they still haven't made a move. This situation needs to be addressed immediately.

While I was en route to headquarters, I received a call from Dream. The way she was screaming in the phone let me know I needed to get over to Club Bliss immediately. I swear they need to close the damn club down because they are never there like they should be. We definitely need to have a sit-down. It's too much lackluster shit going on. That added with them not telling me about the shootout had me livid. Them hard-headed ass niggas know better than to let the motherfucking streets tell me shit before they do.

"It's about time you made it here, Ms. Gladys!" Dream damn near pulled my arm out of the socket.

"Why the hell is the door locked? It's happy hour."

"I've had two bitches overdose and had to be taken to the hospital. By the grace of God, the paramedics revived their dumb ass. Come up to the office. Sheba has some shit she needs to tell you. I tried to get her to tell me, but she scared. That's why I called you and not Fendi. He would have come in here going ballistic."

"I've been told him that he needed to buckle down on these bitches. You came in here and turned a lot of shit around. At the same time, Fendi's ass is out now, and he needs to do his part. Let's go up here and see what the fuck is going on. Did you get any word on their condition?"

"Buck is on it. I'm telling you, Ms. Gladys, those bitches were off something powerful, and it wasn't Supreme." Hearing that made my ears perk up because who in the fuck had dope in my city.

"What the hell is going on, Sheba?"

"Hear me out, Ms. Gladys, before you start going off.

Earlier this week, Suki and Ki-Ki came in here talking about they got ahold of some good ass coke. Of course, you know I do indulge just to be ready for my dates. They took me over east and that's where we met this nigga named Butch. He's an older cat but paid like a motherfucker. Here is one of his bags. I'm sorry, Dream, I know I promised that I would stop using. It just be hard sometimes. That day was the last day I used. I don't know what that shit is, but it's not cut enough. The moment I snorted that shit, I started convulsing and having a seizure. When I woke up, I was in the hospital. They told me that I had to be revived. The only reason I didn't come clean was because I didn't want to lose my job. Please don't fire me. I promise I'm done with that shit."

I couldn't even focus on her crying. My ass was more so concerned about this nigga Butch. It had been years since I bumped heads with my old nemesis. All the rats are coming out of the woodworks around in this motherfucker. The nigga must have got tired of being in witness protection, which means he's obviously ready to head up to the upper room.

"You're not fired, but I can't have you on the roster addicted to that shit. Get in a rehab program, and I'll make sure to keep it between us. If Fendi finds out your ass is still using, he'll definitely fire you. Go get dressed and head over to the hospital to sit with them dumb bitches."

I was impressed seeing Dream really run this shit like a boss. She was a natural, Gavin was eager to learn, and Miyani caught on fast. My grandsons really had no idea just how dope their women were.

"Thanks for being honest, Sheba. Do you remember where you met the nigga Butch at?"

"Yeah. He hangs out at this barbershop called Headhunters. It's one of those shops where the niggas get lap dances and shit while getting their hair cut."

The wheels in my head started to turn. I needed to go to talk to my grandbabies. It's been a minute since we raised hell.

"Close up for the night, Dream. As a matter of fact, we will close down for the rest of the week just until this shit blows over. In a matter of two weeks, there has been a damn shootout and bitches overdosing. The last thing we need is for the police to find out what the fuck is really going on."

"Fendi is going to go the fuck off if we close down, Ms. Gladys."

"I'm not thinking about his ass. He should be here more than to just drink and bullshit. Tell him to take it up with me. I'll beat his ass if he comes out the side of his neck with me. As a matter of fact, I'm about to have a sit down with them now. I'll tell him myself."

I wasted no time getting out of there and headed to talk with my grandsons. Too much shit was going on, and we weren't up on it. I'm about to get down to the bottom of this shit. As I headed over to headquarters, I made sure to call every last one of their ass. The whole Team Supreme needed to be in attendance.

As I walked inside of Team Supreme Headquarters, I immediately pulled my gun out. The one nigga I vowed to kill on sight was sitting at the conference table with grandchildren.

"Whoa!" Silk said as he stood to his feet while putting his hands up in defeat.

"Give me one motherfucking reason why I shouldn't put a bullet in your head right now?"

"Grandma, chill!" Givenchy said as he walked towards me.

"Don't tell me to chill out! Since when you niggas started sitting with the enemy. This man killed my daughter. I owe it to her to avenge her death. All of a sudden, we're not on the same page with murking this motherfucker! Y'all got me fucked up. Where the fuck is the loyalty?" I gritted.

My grandsons had no idea the level of rage that was flowing through my veins.

"Crazy ass old lady, you know damn well we would never cross you. Put the gun up. He has some shit he needs to say."

"If he's not telling me why the fuck he killed my daughter, we don't have shit to talk about. Y'all don't know this sneaky nigga like I do. He was a coke-addicted, abusive, no good nigga.

"Ms. Gladys, I loved Chanel and my sons. I admit I failed as a husband and a father. At the same time, I'm not the one who did that to Chanel. Did I put my hands on her? Yes, I did. But, killing her was something I could never do. I'm here to clear my name and reunite with my boys. All I need is for you to hear me out."

"You have less than a minute."

"When Chanel was murdered, I wasn't even in town. I hopped on a charter flight that morning out to Miami for a meeting with the distributors. A couple of days before I left, we did have a fight. I found she had been doing business with the nigga, Butch Kassidy. I told her the nigga couldn't be trusted, but of course, Chanel never listened to anybody. She was the queen and what she said went. The last time I talked to her, they were supposed to be meeting up so that he could pay her the money owed.

She was dead before I ever made it back. The FEDS arrested me the moment the charter flight landed back here in the Chi. That's my word. I didn't kill Chanel. The only reason I've been coming around trying to talk with the boys is so we can avenge her death."

Once Silk was done speaking, I sat and let what he said marinate. One thing about me is that I can tell when a person is lying. Silk wasn't. As much as I wanted to kill his ass for putting his hands on Chanel, I can't. Since his ass is here vowing to avenge her death, it's only right I let him in.

"You have one time to move funny, and I'm going to kill your ass. We will be in touch. Right now, we have a Team Supreme meeting, so you can see yourself out."

I was letting the nigga live, but he couldn't know my family business. I still don't trust his bitch ass as far as I can throw him.

"We'll be in touch," G said and escorted him out of the conference room.

"Pour me a double shot of Hennessy, Fendi." I needed a damn drink. It was just too much going on for me.

"Why you didn't ask Prada? He's sitting closer to the liquor cabinet."

"Cause I asked your ass. Now get me something to drink before I beat your ass like I used to."

"Your ass is gone fuck around and break one of them badass hips. I got you, granny." Prada said as he got up and poured my drink.

"What's the emergency? I have to get home to Miyani and the kids."

"I understand that you all have to tend to your families. At the same time, you've placed the Team Supreme family on the backburner. I don't like that. Each one of you knows that handling our business is a must. Now understand I am in no way telling you that the family you've created shouldn't be a priority. I'm simply saying that a balance between family and business is important."

"Damn, grandma! You talking like we slipping or some shit."

"I'm glad you spoke first. Had you been on your shit, you would know that two bitches overdosed at the club, not to mention their getting fucked up off some shit that ain't Supreme. So, yeah, your ass is lacking.

Since we're on the topic of the club, why didn't anyone tell me about the shootout? I had to hear the shit from the streets. Y'all know how I feel about that. Anything that happens with Team Supreme, I need to be the first to know.

Then I walk in here, and Silk is sitting in this mother-fucker! That shit is unacceptable. Just because I'm in retirement don't mean shit. I'm still the Head Bitch in Charge.

Now that we have that out of the way, we need to pull up on Butch.

"The nigga Silk was just talking about?" Givenchy asked.

"Yeah, him. You see, from what I heard from a good source, he's behind the drugs that have our girls overdosing. Not only that, but he's selling product without Team Supreme's permission. I don't know about y'all, but grandma is feeling real disrespected. After hearing what ya punk ass daddy just revealed, I feel like a visit to his spot is well overdue."

"When you want to go to see him? Prada asked.

"I want to do some more intel on his ass before we pull up. Right now I have this situation with Judge Akron that needs to be addressed."

"You just make sure this a business meeting and nothing

else. If I find out that nigga is trying to fuck, I'm going to shoot his ass!" Prada said.

"Grandma got to have a life too, Jody?" Fendi laughed.

"You niggas is stupid. No seriously though, what's up with you and him. It's only right you tell us what's going on," Givenchy spoke as he stepped in front of me.

I was trying to leave, but these little niggas were all in my business.

"I don't have to tell y'all niggas nothing. Get the hell out of my way!" I pushed G hard as hell and walked out of the door. The last thing I needed was them niggas up in my game room. It's certain parts of my life that have to be kept personal. This just happens to be one of those things.

"Thank you for coming, Gladys."

"My pleasure. Thank you for inviting me, Joseph."

He stepped to the side and allowed me to step inside of his home. He had been trying to get me to come and have dinner with him since we had reunited. He has a wife and kids, so this visit was definitely business. If I wanted it to get personal, it definitely could. That nigga be pitching a tent in his pants every time he thinks about me. It's been years since we were together intimately. I know if he gets this older, experienced pussy, his wife would be filing for divorce. That old ass nigga would gladly sign it.

"I still can't believe you're still beautiful as ever after all of these years."

"Thank you. Cut the bullshit. Why did you invite me here?"

"Same old Gladys. Straight to the point with no bullshit."

"Ain't nothing changed about me but the stretch marks on my ass. Let's talk business."

"Come into the dining area. I'm no cook, so I ordered takeout. I hope that's good enough. I know a rich woman like you likes the finer things in life. You've come a long way from those dirt roads and that one-room shack. I'm still in disbelief at how you managed to rise up and become a queen pin. Those mediocre beginnings have nothing on this new life you lead now."

We sat down at the table, and he poured us both a shot of Crown Royal.

"I'm very much still that woman that comes from mediocre beginnings. Those struggles made me the person I am today. Again, fuck all this small talk. Why did you want me to have dinner with you?" This old ass nigga was reaching, and it was pissing me off.

"I need to know what's taking so long with the boys holding their end of the bargain. It's been almost two months since they were released, and nothing has happened. You promised they would do it. I feel like I was bamboozled into letting them out. I understand that they are my grandsons, but a deal is a deal."

I knocked back my shot of Crown digesting what he was saying.

"The funny thing about that is they aren't your grandsons," I spoke with a straight face. This nigga had no idea who he was fucking with.

"What the hell you mean, I'm not their grandfather? I'm Chanel's father!"

"Do you actually think I would have a baby by your country bunkin' ass! You're sitting here trying to remind me of my mediocre beginnings when yours are the same. I left your ass on them back country roads and made a life for myself and my daughter. God rest her beautiful soul."

"What are you trying to say, Gladys?"

"You are not the father! This queen pin used your ass. I would do anything for Givenchy, Prada, and Fendi. You, sir, were just a casualty of war. It be that way sometimes."

"As God is my witness, I'll put you and those criminal ass niggas in jail! You lied to me."

This nigga had jumped up and quickly knocked the entire table over. The moment he tried to lunge at me, I pumped his ass full of bullets. What did he think was going to happen coming at a queen pin as he called me? I don't care what a motherfucker calls me. It's when my grandsons are disrespected I have a problem.

From the moment I walked inside that courtroom and saw him, I knew what needed to be done. This nigga forgot he got me drunk off of moonshine and allowed his friends to took advantage of me. It was easy for me to put the shit on him. Unfortunately, Chanel is a product of incest. My uncle raped me on a regular. I've never told a soul, and I intend on keeping it that way.

"Damn! You were supposed to wait for me to come, Ms. Gladys." Butta said as he walked inside of the house.

I had to at least let him on things. He is the one I know will listen and never question my directives. Unlike my hardheaded ass grandsons. Every damn thing I do they got something to say. Butta does whatever no questions asked. Of course, they tease him about it, but he takes the shit in stride.

"I'm sorry. He tried to kill me."

"Yeah, right! Let's get this cleaned up so that we can get out of here." I grinned slyly at Butta. He knows me so well.

As we cleaned things up, I felt no remorse in my hasty

decision to kill his ass. The nigga was well on his way to trying to blackmail us. It was in his demeanor and the shit he said when we spoke. He consistently referred to Team Supreme as a drug cartel and me as a queen pin. Those words alone were suspect to me. I like to nip my family problems in the bud before they get out of control. I didn't have to tell Butta to keep this shit to himself. He already knows how this shit goes.

11

FENDI

I got on my shit fast after my granny got on a nigga about slacking. My ass was making my presence felt more at the club. The more time I spent there, I realized just how much Dream had turned my shit around. Man, she was the realest for getting my properties in order. I knew that things had turned around. I just didn't have an idea of how much they did. By being at the club more, I had been able to sit around and go through the books. We were making money abundantly. It was because of Dream that the shit was legit. Who knew my thieving ass baby would turn shit around for a nigga?

"Why are you smoking in my office, Fendi?"

"Last time I checked, this was my damn office. How the fuck are you going to just take my shit?"

Dream's ass had turned my office into some girly shit. What used to be a *Scarface* themed office was now Marilyn Monroe.

"Fendi, don't come in here changing shit around. This is my office now. Go find one of the empty rooms and make it yours. Put that damn weed out in my office I don't want that smell in here."

Dream was doing too much walking around spraying all that damn air freshener. She had killed my damn vibe acting like didn't smoke like a damn chimney.

"Ain't this about a bitch? A nigga goes to jail and comes home to a hostile takeover. I expect this shit from the niggas in the street, not my woman."

"You're so dramatic. I love you, though." Dream leaned over and kissed me on the lips.

"I love you too, baby. Where's my daughter?"

"She's at home with Ms. Paulette. I just came here to check on everything since we just opened back up after that bullshit. Had I known you were here I would have stayed in bed. I haven't been feeling good these last couple of days."

She looked exhausted as she sat on my lap.

"What's wrong? You don't feel hot or anything."

"I know. It may just be a flu bug or something. I'm going to head back home and lay down."

Looking at Dream, I knew something was off. I kind of felt like she may be pregnant but decided to keep it to myself. Dream was in denial like a motherfucker. I had been all up in them guts raw. It didn't matter how many times she went off about my dumping my seeds off in that pussy. I did it anyway. It was time for her to give me a son. A nigga already had the perfect princess, and it was time for my prince to join the family.

"Butta and Gunna are here keeping an eye on the floor, so I can head home with you if you want."

"Nah, it's okay, babe. I'll see you when you get home."

"Make sure you sleep naked. When I come home, I want to climb up in my pussy."

"Yes, sir!" She saluted me and walked out of the office.

After smoking another blunt, I headed downstairs to join Butta and Gunna. The moment I made it down to the floor, I spotted the last person I wanted to see, a bitch named Shaena I fucked with heavy prior to finding out about my daughter. I stopped fucking with the bitch cold turkey the moment Dream came into my life. This hoe was fifty types of crazy, and I was in no mood to kill this hoe.

"Who the fuck let her in here?" I asked Gunna.

"Dream hired new security, so they didn't know. I didn't want to cause a scene knowing sis was in the building."

"Good looking out. Let me go try to get rid of this bitch. Dream's got this club sewed up like a motherfucker. The last thing I need is someone telling her about this bitch.

"Good luck with that rabid animal." Butta laughed.

I took a deep breath and headed over to the section where she and her crew were. Shaena was the type of bitch that would make you knock her the fuck out like a nigga.

"Let me talk to you for a minute!" I didn't give her a chance to say anything. I yoked the bitch up quick.

"Get your hands off of me, Fendi. Why the fuck are you manhandling me?"

"What the fuck I tell you about being on bullshit?"

"I'm not here on bullshit. Nigga, I'm not even thinking about your no-good ass. It's my girl birthday and her party is here tonight. I was not missing her birthday party on the account of you. I don't care if this is your club, nigga!"

"Make me beat your ass, Shae?"

"Go ahead, Fendi! It's not like you haven't put your hands on me before. Your ass is walking around trying to make it seem like I'm crazy. If I'm crazy, it's because you made me that way. All of a sudden you find out you have a daughter with that hoe, and I'm the problem. You stopped fucking with me out of the blue. I did nothing to you, Fendi.

Why are you doing this to me? Does that bitch know about me? Did you tell her I was smuggling shit in my pussy for you? I risked my freedom for years for your ass and you dropped my ass like a bad habit. I was pregnant by your ass three times, and you made me kill it. This bitch stole from you and turned up with a baby by you. I would never do that to you Fendi, and you know that."

Shaena was crying, and of course, I felt bad because she was telling the truth. However, the heart wants what the heart wants. It just so happens that my heart is with Dream.

"I'm sorry, Shae. Shit wasn't working out with us. My heart is with Dream. We have a family now, and I can't fuck that up. You've been compensated for anything you've ever done that caused you to risk your freedom. Again, I'm sorry shit didn't work out, but I simply can't have you here. You have to go, Shaena."

"You love that hoe so much, but do you know how many dicks that bitch had in her mouth before she met you? I've been waiting for the moment to burst your bubble. Look at your precious Dream. That bitch was taking dick in all holes. You got this hoe running shit for you, and she's a known thot. Do you see the nigga she fucking in the video?"

Taking a closer look at the video Shae was showing me, I almost lost my cool, but I couldn't do it in front of her bitch ass. It was without a doubt Dream and this fuck nigga Ceno I had beefed with over the years.

"Send that to my phone."

"That will be a thousand dollars nigga. This shit ain't free!"

"Bitch, I'll put a bullet in your head right now! Send that shit to me now!" I had pulled my gun out and put it up to her head. Right now was the wrong fucking time to play with a nigga.

Once she sent the shit, I let her go. The video had me sick to my stomach. Yeah, I was fully aware of what Dream did prior to us getting together but porn was never discussed. Watching them niggas take turns fucking her had me disgusted with her ass. The last thing I wanted to do was look at her ass.

When I made it home, she was in bed asshole naked just like I requested. A nigga dick couldn't get hard after seeing that video. I slept in the guest bedroom instead of in our bed. Yeah, a nigga was fucked up behind this shit.

"ARE YOU HUNGRY, bae? I made breakfast for you." Dream was standing over the kitchen stove naked with nothing but an apron on.

"Nah, I'm straight. I'll eat at my granny's joint."

"Since when you don't want my French toast?"

"Since I'm not hungry!" I banged my fist on the table, not being able to control my anger.

The flashbacks were driving me crazy, and I wanted to kill her ass. It didn't matter that the shit happened before our time. Dream's just so damn beautiful. Knowing she subjected herself as a woman to be treated like a slut has me pissed.

"Who the fuck pissed in your corn flakes, nigga? I suggest you pipe the fuck down, yelling at me."

Dream cut the stove off and walked out of the kitchen. Of course, I followed right behind her ass. Before she could even touch the bottom of the staircase, I grabbed her by all of that horse hair. I made sure to wrap it around my hand tight. A nigga tried to break her fucking neck. I had her head pulled back so that she could see that I wasn't playing with her ass.

"Watch your mouth, whore!"

"What is wrong with you, Fendi? Let me go." She was trying to squirm away from me, but I held on tighter.

"Did you tell that nigga Ceno to let you go when he had his dick in your mouth? Bitch, I saw the video of you letting them niggas take turns fucking you! Them niggas had their dick in your mouth. The same mouth you put on my daughter and me." The sound of our daughter crying should have made me let her hair go, but it didn't.

"W-w-what! W-w-wait! Fendi, please! I can explain. Just please let my hair go!"

"There ain't shit to explain. Bitch, I saw the video." I wanted to slap the fuck out of Dream so bad. Instead, I bit the fuck out of her ass on her neck.

"Ahhhhhhhh! Stop it, Fendi. Chanel is crying!" she screamed, and finally, I let her go.

She rushed up the stairs and fell in the process, but she got up quickly and raced inside of our daughter's room. I was right on her ass because this shit wasn't over. Our daughter was no longer crying once she picked her up. She tried to walk out of the room, but I blocked her ass.

"Did that nigga Ceno send you here to set me up?" I gritted.

"No. I would never set you up. Come on now, Fendi! You know I love you."

"Is that the same thing you were telling that nigga? What you let them niggas fuck you at the same time for money? If you lie, I swear to God I'm going to forget you're the mother of my daughter and beat your ass."

"Yes, I fucked them for the money, but I didn't know I

was being videotaped until afterwards. Please, Fendi you have to believe me!"

"Why the fuck should I believe a liar and a thief?"

"I'm sorry!"

"Keep that shit. I can't believe I'm in love with a whore! Let me get the fuck outta here before I murk ya!"

Dream grabbed my shirt, but I quickly knocked her hand away.

"Really, Fendi! You promised me my past didn't matter! That shit happened before your time! Please don't do this to me! We've been doing so good. Don't leave Fendi, just please let me explain!" Dream was really crying, and a part of me felt like shit. The other part was angry as fuck seeing them niggas with my baby. I just can't get those images out of my head.

"I need some time to digest this shit, ma. This shit really got me fucked up. Just give me some space, that's all I ask." Before walking away, I kissed my daughter on the forehead.

"If you walk out without letting me explain, I won't be here when you come back."

"Who said I'm coming back?"

Lord knows I didn't mean that, but the threat of her saying that shit angered me. I felt the urge to hit her, but I was already wrong for the way I disrespected her. Instead, I made sure to get the fuck out of the house. Things had already got out of hand.

12
____

DREAM

Numb was the only word to describe the way I was feeling. My heart felt empty behind this shit with Fendi. It had been a week, and he had yet to come back home. He called all day and every day to check on Chanel. That was cool with me. I'm glad he at least still cared for her. As hurt and upset that I am behind the way Fendi treated me, I could never involve our daughter.

I had yet to leave the home Fendi and I shared. At first, I was serious about leaving. The more I thought about it, the more I knew not to leave. I changed my entire life for this man. Fuck that! I earned my spot in this mansion. He could stay gone for all I give a fuck. I'm still going to rock my position like the boss bitch I am. I still have access to all the nigga's money, so he ain't that damn mad.

I'm not going to front, though, him not coming back since that day has me in my feelings. This shit so embarrassing I haven't told anyone. Miyani was on such a high from getting engaged that I refused to rain on her parade. She enough on her plate. The last thing she needed was my crybaby ass putting a damper on my happiness. I hadn't said anything to Gavin either. There was no way I could seek comfort with Ms. Gladys. Although she fucked with me heavy, I had to deal with this one on my own. At the end of the day, Fendi is still her grandson, so, of course, she will be on his side.

No matter what, I'm still that bitch Dream. I don't beg niggas to do anything when it comes to me. Had our daughter not been involved, I would have been cleaned his ass out and kept it the fuck moving. It doesn't help that this nigga has made me fall in love with him. I've never been in love, and this is the reason why. Niggas will switch up on you the minute some shit doesn't go their way. The nigga is not fooling me. Fendi is hurt behind seeing me fucking them niggas.

I was paid ten thousand dollars for a threesome. What bitch in their right mind would pass that up? My only question was who wanted to go first. I wouldn't tell Fendi that, though. He would really kill me if he knew how down I was for the shit. Back then, it sounded like a good idea. The shit backfired when I learned about the tape. Ceno promised me that the shit would never get out. Now that nigga owes me money because I paid his ass to delete the shit.

~

"To what do I owe this visit?" Ceno asked as I walked inside of his car wash.

"Nigga, you know why the fuck I'm here! You owe me ten thousand dollars with your bitch ass. Why would you leak that fucking tape? Somebody showed that shit to my man."

"Wait a minute! Slow the fuck down. I didn't do no shit like that!"

"Then how the fuck did it get out!"

"I showed it to him."

I turned around at the sound of a female's voice. Anger came over me. It was the same bitch I bumped into at the jail when I went to see Fendi.

"Shaena! What the fuck? Why would you do that shit?" Ceno was heated.

I breathed a sigh of relief knowing he didn't do that shit, but who was this bitch and how did she get a hold to it?

"I'm sorry, Ceno! I had to show Fendi so that he could know what he was dealing with. This shit is not fair. How do I just sit back and let him love her? He makes me get an abortion with all my babies, but she pops up with a baby, and now he's in love. No! I refuse to accept it."

This crazy bitch was unraveling right before my eyes, and everything was so fucking clear. Fendi lied to me about that bitch. I had every intention of fucking him up behind this one. That man looked me right in the eye and lied to me. He had a lot of nerve the way he was walking around behaving with me.

"Who is this bitch, Ceno?"

"Man, Dream, this my cousin Shaena. I'm sorry. I fucked up. Bitch, you talk too much. I distinctly told your ass not to go repeating that shit."

"Fuck her! She doesn't deserve him. How does it feel to be a single parent now, you cum guzzling hoe? That nigga doesn't want you or that baby. For all we know, she could be any nigga's baby in the city. I mean, you do be around this motherfucker passing out that pussy to the highest bidder. When Fendi is done finding out about your ass, he's going to run right into my arms."

I was trying my best not to laugh at this fucked up looking female. The outdated red bottoms and fake ass Chanel purse let me know the struggle was real. Poor tink,

tink was about to lose her mind looking at me wearing all Fendi's money. She wanted my life and was willing to do anything to get it. Too bad for her, I wasn't coming up off of Fendi period!

"Are you retarded or something, bitch? What makes you think I'm a single parent? The only thing you did was made that man love me more. He just about lost his mind behind that shit. My baby is so mad he might be on his way to kill Ceno and his brother ass right now. Since you know so much, let me enlighten you, hoe. Hoe, do you see this chain around my neck? Do you see that Bentley outside? I already know you follow me on IG, so I'm sure you see our home. Hoe, understand that nigga loves my pussy even on the bloody days. You could never be me. Maybe if you had robbed his ass like I did, he might have some respect for you. Bitch, you ain't good enough for nothing but moving pills in your pussy while I move weight across the city. We are not the same. You don't fuck him better than me, you don't love him more than me, and you for damn sure don't pray for him better than me. I'm going to let that comment you said about my child slide because you don't know any better. I'm not going to give any warnings to you, bitch. Just know I'll put a bullet in your ass for trying to fuck up my family which you can't fuck up?"

"I'm not scared of you, Dream! Or should I call your ass a nightmare? That's exactly what your ass is going to be for my man Fendi! When I'm done exposing your ass, he'll never love you." I had to pinch my nose to calm down because this hoe thought I was playing with her ass.

"Ceno, you better put a muzzle on this mutt."

"Come on now, Shaena! Get off this bullshit I don't need that shit around here."

"Fuck that hoe! Ahhhhhhhhhh!"

That triggered the fuck out of me, so I pulled out my gun and shot her ass in each leg. I didn't come here for all of this bullshit. At the same time, I'm glad I did because now I know where Fendi got the damn video from.

"Next time, it will be in your fucking head! My nigga will be to see you, Ceno, so I suggest you get rid of the fucking tape."

I placed on my Dolce & Gabbana shades and walked out cool as fuck, just like I walked in. My next stop was Team Supreme Headquarters. Fendi Alexander had me fucked all the way up!

Not even ten minutes into my drive over there, Fendi started blowing my phone up. I guess his bitch called and told him I shot her ass. He sent a text talking about bring my ass home. I laughed all the way to the crib cause now the nigga was at the crib. At first, I had the right mind not to go home and make him wait for me. I decided not to, though. This nigga had some explaining to do. As I drove, I made sure to remove all my jewelry so that it wouldn't get broke. I'm going in ready to fight this crazy motherfucker. It took me about twenty minutes to make it to the house. Of course, when I walked inside Fendi was waiting on my ass.

"What the fuck I tell you about not answering the phone for me?"

"Oh! I'm supposed to answer the phone for you. Last time I checked, you've been MIA for a week. Where the fuck were you at?"

"This is not about me, Dream! Sit the fuck down because you're too damn hype. I'm not in the mood for this shit today!"

I fell out laughing. This nigga had nerves.

"I'm not in the mood, but I got motherfucking time!" I stepped out of my Jimmy Choo's and pounced on his ass.

"What the fuck? I'm not playing Dream! Ahhhhh! Stop biting me!" I was trying to bite a chunk out of his face. The nigga bit the fuck out of me earlier this week, and I vowed to get my bite back. When he came and showed me the video, I wasn't given the opportunity to explain. That shit hurt my soul, but after finding out that bitch was behind it, I'm angry. This nigga gon' have to fight me.

I started shaking with his cheek in my mouth like a Pitbull.

"Ahhhhhhhhhhh!" Fendi was yelling, and I didn't stop until I tasted blood. Then I started throwing every vase and statue I could find.

"You got me fucked up! That bitch showed you that video. Nigga, you looked me in my face and lied to me when you were locked up! She was more than some bitch transporting drugs, Fendi! You were fucking her.

"I didn't lie to you! That was why she was there! On my motherfucking daughter, the moment we became one, I cut the bitch off! I'm a beat your ass if you throw something else!"

"Let's rumble nigga! When it's all said and done, we're definitely going to be in this motherfucking humbugging! How dare you not let me explain myself? Your ass hasn't been home for a week. As far as I'm concerned, you could stay gone forever! While you're at it, order ya hoe a wheelchair. I'm sure you know I hit the hoe in her legs. I will not deal with disrespect of any kind. Not from you and most definitely not a bitch you used to fuck. In my opinion, if it's fuck me, then it's fuck you, nigga!" I made sure to mush him upside the damn head.

"You're so fucking dramatic, Dream!"

"I'm not dramatic nigga. You knew about my past when we made shit official. The first time something from my past pops up, your ass starts going off. That shit is not fair to me, Fendi!" I was trying my best to hold in how hurt I really was. I'm feisty, but I have feelings too.

"What the fuck you expect me do? That shit fucked me up seeing you with them niggas. I don't want to see no nigga fucking my future wife!"

"Awww! You want me to be your wife." I moved closer to where he was standing.

"Hell yeah! I love you and my daughter, Dream. In my head, I'm the only nigga that had that pussy! That video did nothing but remind me that I'm not. Why the fuck would you do some shit like that?" he gritted.

Looking at him, I could tell he was more hurt than anything.

"I'm not proud of it. You're acting as if I walk around bragging about the shit. My only focus is the new life I have. Having a baby changed my entire existence. Meeting you changed me. If it's any consolation you, treat me better than any man I've ever been with. Stop thinking about how other niggas have been with me. You and I share something that we don't share with anybody else. That's our daughter Chanel and the baby that I'm carrying now."

Fendi's eyes lit up like a Christmas tree. He had got me pregnant, which was what he was trying to do from the jump.

"Really? You pregnant again by a nigga?" Fendi grabbed me and rubbed on my stomach.

"Yeah. I took a test but never got a chance to tell you. Your ass was so mad behind the video that you spoiled the moment. Honestly, I'm not sure if I'm ready to be a mother of two so soon. One thing I am sure of is that I love the family that we have created. So, if that means I have to be walking around here pregnant with a two-year-old, then so be it. We can have a beautiful family. The shit won't work if you're worried about my past, Fendi. Lord knows I don't give a fuck about yours! What you did before me is none of my concern. I can't fault you for what happened prior to us getting together. I have to accept you for the great man you are to our daughter and me. What you did to me was unfair. I didn't deserve to be called a whore. If you ever fix your mouth to call me that again, I'll shoot you like I just shot that bitch."

"I swear I'm going to shoot ya ass back. Why the fuck would you do that? Now I have to do damage control."

"You don't have to do a motherfucking thing. That bitch was running her dick suckers about me. I gave her fair warning. I also told Ceno's bitch ass you were on the way to fuck him up. Let's go kick his ass right now! His ass is the reason all of this shit is happening anyway

"That's how I know about the shit. He hit me up, trying to explain himself. I told that nigga to get the fuck out of dodge and take that hoe with him before I murk both of their dumb asses. I can't believe your ass is out here on bullshit while you're pregnant. Sit your ass down somewhere."

"I had to do what I had to do. My relationship is in jeopardy behind this shit. This is the happiest I've ever been in my life, and I'm not about to just lose it all, not without a fight anyway. Come here. Your face is bleeding."

"Hell, nah! Don't touch me with your crazy violent ass." Fendi yanked away, and I held in my laughter.

He headed up the stairs, and I followed right behind him. Fendi walked inside the bathroom, and I stood in the doorway watching him as he placed a hot towel up to his face.

"Were you serious about wanting me to be your wife?"

"I've never been so serious about anything in my entire

life. After the way you're crazy ass just attacked my ass, I'm having second thoughts."

"Just call it even. Since we've met, you put your hands on me twice. It's only right I get a chance to kick your ass nigga. I really do love you, Fendi."

"I know you love me. Man, Dream, a nigga loves the fuck out of you too. It's just scary for me. Love and relationships have never been my thing, but you make a nigga want both. Now that we're building a family, anything that threatens it makes me go crazy."

"I feel the same way. I'm willing to kill anything moving when it comes to my happiness. With you is where I find my happy place. Let's kiss and make up."

"Hell nah! You think you can come in here whooping on my ass and we're supposed to be cool."

This nigga was really in his feelings. I swear these tough ass niggas cannot take what they dish out. He's lucky I'm tired of fighting with his ass. These hormones got me horny as hell.

"Fuck it! Let me give you some of this Jilly from Philly!"

"What the fuck is you talking about?"

"Relax! You know I'm a pro at rocking the mic."

I dropped down to my knees and started giving him the best head he ever had. It's safe to say that nigga forgot why he was mad at me.

13

MIYANI

Since G's proposal, I had been on such a high. My baby had me feeling like the luckiest woman in the world. Every chance I got, I was showing off my ring and referring to him as my fiancé. Gavin and Dream were sick of my shit, but I didn't give a fuck. I couldn't wait to walk down the aisle and officially take that man's last name. I was more than ready since all my life I lived with the name Mills. Gavin is going to be so mad when I finally do tell her about her sick ass momma.

Honestly, I put her revelation in the back of my mind and carried on. I needed to focus on my new life. It had been a month since G gave me the keys to the dance studio. I immediately hired a crew and started to work on it. I couldn't wait for my girls to see their new space. Gianna was going to be so excited. Dance has become so important to her. She lives, eats, and breathes it. I literally have to make her stop wearing her costumes everywhere.

Since giving birth, it had been hard to really get out and help Givenchy. He would much rather me be at home with the kids these days, which is okay with me. I have no complaints. It's just that when he was away, I handled shit. Now that he's home he's acting like he don't need me. I'm not going to lie. I miss negotiating and closing business deals. Nevertheless, I'm happy I accomplished the one thing he couldn't due to him being locked up, which was the Chanel House and Supreme Suites. We would be cutting the ribbon on them in a couple of days. It was a red carpet event for the whole family.

Givenchy was so excited. This was a personal accomplishment for him and I'm so glad I was able to help get it done. The entire Alexander family was getting ready to show the fuck up and show out. The city is definitely not ready for Supreme Suites. A lot of dope boyz were about to be out of business. Givenchy's a damn genius for making that shit a modern-day Carter. The board of directors had no clue what they had endorsed. It was my job to sell their ass a dream. They bought it and now my man is about to have the whole city bowing down to Team Supreme.

After a long night of fucking, both Givenchy and I were exhausted. The sound of his phone continuously going off was irritating me. During the night, I had to put G-Baby in bed with us with his crybaby ass. I'm so mad we spoiled him. He won't sleep unless he is close to one of us. I quickly grabbed the phone to silence it. Whoever it is was about to get cursed the fuck out if they wake up my man or my baby. G is always gone, so I take full advantage of the days when he sleeps in.

As I grabbed his phone, a text came through. I knew I shouldn't have looked at it, but in my defense, it was already in my hand. It was from the bitch India. It took everything inside of me not to call the bitch and go off. She had sent him so many pictures of them. The pictures were before my time but the one that pissed me off was her asshole naked. I was definitely about to see this bitch. The more I looked through the phone the more I realized she had been sending him all types of shit. Luckily for him, he had left the bitch on read. My baby hadn't responded to any of the hoe advances. Clearly she was losing her mind. She went from trying to seduce him to threatening his life. She had me fucked up. I needed to have a sit-down with the hoe.

After silencing the ringer, I laid in bed staring at the ceiling. All of my life people have tried to play with me. I've always been a nice person, but for some reason, people think it's sweet. Looking over at my future husband, I knew I had to start moving differently. He's the type of man that wants to fight my battles for me. Being a part of Team Supreme requires that I have to handle shit on my own. Putting shit on the back burner and acting as if it didn't happen is not good. It's time I address shit head-on. Each moment I wait to react gives people even more of a reason to think it's okay to play with me. I'm really done playing with everybody around this motherfucker.

"DAMN, baby! You look good as fuck! I've never seen you dressed like that. You dressed like you're about to do a murder." Givenchy grabbed me by the waist and pulled me close.

I had on a black Christian Dior catsuit with some matching boots. My brand new black mink Sable coat set it off just right. It was wintertime in the Chi, so I was dressed for the weather.

"I have a business lunch with some developers for the dance studio."

My heart raced as I spoke the words. I had just lied to Givenchy, and it didn't feel good. I could just say I'm about to confront your rat ass baby momma. If I did that, I knew that he would stop. I'm making an executive decision for the greater good of Team Supreme. I'm taking his advice and running with it. My chin is up, and my chest is out to fuck India up if she plays with me today.

"Hurry up home! I have a surprise for you when you come home."

"Well, let me hurry up. You know I love surprises, my love." We exchanged a deep kiss, and I headed out of the door.

As I headed over to this bitch India's house, I felt like I should tell someone where I was going. I just didn't want to risk G finding out. That and I didn't want anyone trying to talk me out of going. This hoe needed to understand I'm not going anywhere. She needed to get the fuck ASAP!

IT TOOK me about an hour to get to her address. I knew where she lived because I used to drop Gianna off for visits. That was before G stopped her from visiting the crazy ass bitch. Without hesitating, I headed straight up to her door. The door opened before I could ring the bell.

"Does Givenchy know that you're here?" she asked with a sarcastic laugh.

"No, he doesn't. We need to have a talk woman-to-woman." She stood to the side and invited me in.

"Listen, sweetie. I don't do the whole Barbara and Shirley thing. We know Givenchy your man. I'm good. I had the dick already. You want to hit this?" This bitch flamed up a blunt and sat down on the couch. Yeah, I could see me fucking her up in here.

"Let's be clear I'm not here on no Barbara and Shirley type of shit. My man is not checking for you, periodt! However, for some reason, you think it's okay to send him nudes and old pictures of y'all. Yeah, you were with him before me and gave him his first child. At the same time, you're a police ass bitch, and he hates your guts. The history, the bond you had, the fact that you birthed his seeds holds no weight. Sweetie, you're a rat. Deal with the consequences of your actions and stop playing with my man."

"That chain got you feeling like a boss bitch!" She smirked as she blew smoke in the air.

"I am a boss bitch! This chain doesn't mean shit. What's your point, India? No, let me rephrase that. What the fuck is your motive? Why are you back here? All of a sudden, you show up with the police and have them arrested. Now all of a sudden you're not the police anymore. I find it hard to believe that you don't have an ulterior motive. What's it going to take for you to disappear again?"

India leaned all the way back on the sofa and continued to smoke on the blunt. The seconds of silence were extremely awkward. While staring at the hoe, I took notice of the lighter she had previously lit her blunt with. It was a beautiful diamond-encrusted monogram lighter. The lighter stood out to me because I knew who that belonged to. It was my mother's lighter. Gavin and I had that made for her about two years ago for Christmas. How in the fuck did she get it? I knew that my mother advocated for this hoe, but I thought it was because she hated the Alexander family. Something definitely wasn't adding up.

"I don't have an ulterior motive. Gianna is my daughter,

and I deserve to be in her life! G is keeping her from me, and I'm not giving up that easy!"

"Your ass is a clown. You gave up easy the moment you allowed the government to make you walk out on your nigga and daughter. Where was this tough ass energy then? It's obvious talking to you is a waste of my fucking time. Just stop sending shit to my nigga's phone. Givenchy and I are about to get married, and I will be in Gianna's life. Nothing will change that."

India started clapping and staring at me like she was crazy.

"That nigga got you walking around this city like you run shit. Newsflash, sweetie, you don't. Stop trying to act like you're some gangsta bitch! Stick to wearing tutus and dancing on the tops of your toes. That's a better fit. Mya, please go home and finish living the life that's rightfully mine."

"Now we're getting somewhere. That's why you big mad, huh? You feel like I'm living your life! Please wake the fuck up, India. I'm living the life Givenchy wants me to have. It has nothing to do with you. That fine ass man you left walked inside of my dance studio with the daughter you share. That nigga fell in love at the very sight of me. Your daughter loves me because I'm everything you're not. You around here acting like you're back here to be in your daughter's life. Bitch, you don't want to be a parent. Gianna is nothing but a pawn in your game against Givenchy. He doesn't want you, and he never will. Let me give you some words of advice and fair warning. Please move around and find you something safe to do. You will never ever have Givenchy and Gianna the way you had them prior to abandoning them. Cut your losses and walk the fuck away."

"I love how you think you know me so well. You see, my

return here is bigger than Givenchy and my daughter. Be clear they are on my agenda because we have unfinished business. However, I recently connected with my birth mother. We're getting to know each other." She winked and grinned at me with a familiar sinister smile.

It all hit me like a ton of bricks, but I held my composure.

"Well, whatever the reason is, you're here. Stay the fuck away from my family. This is my first and last time speaking on it."

"Whatever you say, Mya, see your way out."

"It kills you to speak my name. Don't worry. Your baby daddy screams it loudly every night." I laughed at her ass and walked out of her house.

Jumping in my car, I knew I should have been going home, but I needed to talk with Dream and Gavin about this shit. I had to tell someone else this shit to ensure I wasn't reaching. All of a sudden, she's here reuniting with her birth mother. Why has that never been said prior to today? I couldn't even get to meet up with Gavin and Dream because Givenchy started blowing my phone. That snitch ass bitch couldn't wait to tell on me.

"Before you go off on me, just let me explain." I was in full defense mode as I walked inside of G's office at home. He had his index finger pressed up against his temple, so I knew he was mad.

"I'm not about to go off on you, but I do want to know why you went over to India's without talking with me first. I don't give a fuck about her. I'm more concerned about you.

She's not to be trusted, beautiful." He flamed up a blunt and hit a couple of times before handing it to me.

I removed my mink coat and sat down across from him. I took a couple of pulled from the blunt and handed it back to him.

"I knew that you would stop me from going. This time I needed to make an executive decision. I'm sorry, G, but I don't like the way India is moving. After confronting that bitch today, I really don't trust that bitch. This morning, while we were sleeping, your phone was going off. In an effort to keep it from waking you and G-Baby up, I turned off the ringer. In the midst of me doing that, messages came through from her. I'm not feeling her sending you nudes and old ass pictures of y'all. Trust me. I'm not worried about it because you belong to me. At the same time, I needed to confront her ass about the disrespect. It took everything inside of me not to fight her ass. Something did stand out to me that she said, though."

I paused, gathering what I was about to say to him.

"What was that?"

"She basically said that besides being here for Gianna, she was here getting to know her birth mother. While there, I took notice of a lighter that was on her coffee table. It was my mother's lighter. How did she get that lighter? Gavin and I brought her that lighter for Christmas a couple of years ago. I don't know. Maybe I'm reaching. After my mother basically praised India like she knew her, I think she's her birth mother."

G took long pulls from the blunt as he walked over to his safe. He typed in the code, and it opened. He went inside and grabbed a folder.

"Here, look at this."

I stared at him intensely before looking at the contents

of the folder. The first thing that stood out to me was a birth certificate. Just like I expected, it was India's and my mother's name was on there as the mother. There was no information in regard to the father. I continued to thumb through the paperwork, and her adoption records were in there as well.

"All of this is absolutely crazy. How did you get a hold to this? Why aren't you just telling me about this?"

"You've had enough on your plate. Plus, from the moment I got out, I've been trying to figure out why the fuck India was back. This is a big part of why I've been keeping Gianna away from her. Just knowing that Melissa is her mother is all the more reason why my daughter will never be around that bitch. Not only that, but I hired a private investigator who helped me secure these documents. Keep looking through them. There is more."

I shook my head, wondering what more could there possibly be to this bullshit. The birth certificate alone had me sick to my stomach. There is no way that hoe India is my sister. I definitely couldn't wait to talk to my sister about this shit.

As I looked at the rest of the documents, my eyes widened, looking at my mother's police record. She had done time for embezzlement, credit card fraud, and prostitution. The worse part of all the charges was that she was a known madam.

"Is this shit real, babe? My mother was a madam back in the day. How in the hell does my father not know any of this?"

"He knows all of it. Who do you think made sure to get that shit sealed? Your father is not as innocent as he tries to be. He just tries to save face for you and Gavin. I've been doing business with your father for some time now, beautiful."

"Are you still doing business with him?"

"No. The moment his actions hurt you, I cut ties. That added with your mother getting in nigga's business, it was imperative that I took a step back. I couldn't afford for my family to be caught up in a political scandal. Plus, I want nothing to do with anybody that makes you cry. Trust me. They will pay for hurting you. What do you want to do with all of this? I've just been holding on to it, not too sure about what to do. Bullets can end all of this shit easily. At the same time, I feel like you and Gavin need to confront this shit head-on for the closure you need. Your mother owes both of you an explanation. We both know she won't give you one, so this is totally your call. We can keep the information and save it for when we need it as leverage. It doesn't matter either way with me. My concern is you and how this makes you feel."

G stood up and walked over to where I was sitting. He pulled me up out of the chair and wrapped his arms around me. The idea that this man felt that it was important to include me in everything makes me love him more and more every day.

"Thank you for loving me so much. I've never been loved this way. Every night before I lay my head down to sleep, I pray three times, once for me, once for our family, and a special one just for you. I never want to live without you, so I make sure to let God know how much I need you. As far as this information, I want to confront them. Baby, I'm not expecting anything major to come from this. I just want to know why they have lied to me my entire life. I've always been a good kid growing up. I'm not so much mad at my father. It's my mother and her bullshit. It's still mindboggling how she's team India all of a sudden. She gave her up for adoption, and they just got reunited. How does my mother go from loving me to hating me? It's as if she's replaced her love for me and given it to India. Truthfully, the shit doesn't even hurt anymore. I'm more confused than anything."

"Melissa doesn't love anybody but herself. She's a liar, a thief, and a fraud. Those types of people always looking for their next victim. India is desperate for some type of family, so she's blinded by the obvious. Your mother has formed a relationship with India because they're now running a sex trafficking ring. That's why my daughter cannot and will not ever go to her house again. I've been keeping a watchful eye and ear on her ass. Look at this."

Givenchy pulled out his phone and started letting me listen to the audio of my mother and India. He pulled up videos from inside of her house, and I couldn't believe it.

"You are a genius, baby."

"Team Supreme always stays ten steps ahead of the enemy. You need to have a sit-down with Gavin and decide when you want to talk to your parents. Remember not to let them know that you know everything. I don't have to tell you how to carry the conversation. Talk less and listen more. Now take that shit off, I like you better when you're naked."

G knocked everything off his desk in one swipe. I wish y'all could see me coming up out of my clothes. This nigga was definitely going to have me pregnant again with all this fucking.

~

"Bitch, this food is so damn good. We need to come out to eat more often." Dream said as she placed a piece of steak inside of her mouth.

"I swear. Prada don't let me eat too much of shit. The house is full of healthy shit, which is fine, but sometimes a bitch be wanting a Double Quarter Pounder with bacon, cheese, and mac sauce." I fell out laughing listening to her greedy ass.

"Well, you bitches know that I always eat healthy. I have Givenchy eating healthier as well. Ms. Gladys was mad as hell when she made pork shoulder, and he turned it down. Talking about I'm changing her baby. That lady knows she's so overprotective of them demons she calls grandsons.

"That old lady is crazy ass fuck. I changed the locks on my house. I'm tired of waking up to her in my house cooking. Do y'all know she was cooking deer stew last week in my kitchen? That shit had my house stinking for days. That was the final straw. I got sick as fuck watching Fendi fuck that stew up. I could only wonder what that woman fed them growing up."

I observed Dream fucking her food up damn near about to choke herself.

"Slow down before you choke yourself, bitch!"

"I'm glad you said something. Your ass is eating like you're pregnant," Gavin added.

"I was going to wait until after my first check-up this week, but since you hoes in my business. Yes, I'm pregnant."

"Yassssss! Congratulations, friend, I'm so happy for you!" I screamed as I reached across the table and hugged her.

"Congratulations, Dream! I know Fendi is happy as hell," Gavin added.

"Yeah, he is. I'm just glad we made up because that video had that nigga going crazy."

"Yeah, me too. Your ass don't have any more videos floating around, do you?" I just had to ask. After finding out about the video, I was so mad. I always told Dream ass some of that shit was going to come back to bite her in the ass.

"Shit, if it is, I don't know anything about it."

"Bitch, it better not be! You had Fendi crying. Don't tell him I told you. Prada will kick my ass if he knows that I told you."

We all laughed just hearing that big bad Fendi was shedding tears was hilarious. I observed Gavin grab her phone and quickly put it away angrily. Her smile changed to a somber look.

"What's wrong, sis?"

"Our mother wants me to meet her for lunch tomorrow. She's been asking for a week, and I've yet to respond."

Dream and I locked eyes hearing that. I still hadn't come clean to Gavin about any of the information that I knew. I planned to tell her about it tonight over dinner. Hearing her say that made me hold off from coming clean because I could use that to my advantage.

"Are you going to go?"

"I don't know, sis. I'm just not feeling her shit these days. I do want to see daddy because I miss him so much."

Hearing her say the last line tugged at my heart because I missed him too. He is the only father I've ever known, so my love for him will never change. Of course, I would feel some type of way finding out if he knew I wasn't his.

"Just go. I'm sure he would love to see you and CJ."

"The only way I'll go is if you go with me."

"Nah, I don't think so. I'll fuck around and kill Melissa's ass." I took a sip of my wine and acted as if I wasn't with it, knowing damn well I was down.

"You should go, Miyani. It's definitely time for you to handle that situation accordingly," Dream added.

"Look, I'm going to go, but don't be mad at me if I knock everything over in that house."

"Just know we're walking in that bitch a team and walking out that way, no matter what. If we have to tear that bitch up, then let's do it and move on." Gavin reached across the table and firmly gripped my hand. I was more than ready to confront my parents.

14

GAVIN

After Miyani agreed to accompany me, I responded to my mother's email. Of course, I didn't tell her that she was coming with me. It was obvious she didn't want Miyani to come, which was something I didn't like. Something was wrong with the entire situation. I didn't understand what my mother had against her all of a sudden. We knew she was mad at me for leaving Carlo, but she really didn't have a legit reason to be mad at Miyani.

I'm glad she decided to go with me. It's time for both of us to close this chapter in our lives. We've both moved onto the happiness we deserve, but it hard to just live life as if we don't have parents. The fact that my mother and father have basically gone on as if we don't exist is crazy. It also speaks volumes to me. It hurts, but if they want to cut us off for who we love, then so be it.

After the shit I just went through, I'm not allowing a soul to make me feel bad for choosing Gavin. No woman should be punished for choosing her own happiness over others. I've always chosen everybody else over me and that shit dead. I'll mop the ocean floor before I give anyone the power over me. Melissa and Malcolm Mills better make sure they come all the way correct with me. They will definitely see a side of me that they have never seen before. I'm no longer the old Gavin that they used to know. That's courtesy of them for choosing Carlo over me. Now, they have to deal with me choosing Prada. That and they had better not talk crazy to my sister. Ain't no more of sitting quiet while they treat her bad. She always comes to my rescue, and it's only right I do the same for her.

MIYANI and I sat in the driveway of our childhood home, smoking a fat ass blunt. We were about to step inside of what now feels like hell. Lord knows growing up it didn't feel that way. The only thing that fucked up our childhood up was our over-demanding mother and her need to win. Outside of that, we truly lived good.

"What you think she's going to say about me being here?"

"That old bitch is about to lose her shit, but she'll get over it."

I took a long pull from the blunt and passed it to Miyani. While she hit it, I sent texts back and forth with Prada. He was unaware that I was meeting up with my mother. I would tell him afterwards.

"That's Prada again, huh?"

"Yeah, I told him I was out at a business with you." She exhaled and handed the blunt back to me.

"How are things going on with you two?"

"I guess things are good for the most part. We still haven't discussed him finding out about me taking birth control. It's like he's trying to act as though it didn't happen. I probably wouldn't care if he wasn't about to propose to me. He threw the damn ring in the garbage as if it was nothing. After retrieving it out of the garbage, I placed it in his top drawer. Later that day, I went back, and it was gone. He has never spoken a word about the entire situation since that day. I know that Prada's mind works differently. At the same time, all he does is hold things in. Eventually, he's going to explode. I don't like the fact that he tried to act like certain shit didn't happen. Do you know he saw what happened to his mother and has never told his brothers?"

"Are you serious?"

"Yes, I'm at my wit's end with him popping Percocet like candy. That nigga is unraveling right before my eyes. Prada is big on our personal business staying in our house. That's why I haven't really been speaking on it. He will go nuts if I talk with Givenchy and Fendi about things. As his woman, I'm just trying to be that safe place he needs."

I had to hit the blunt a couple of more times. Just thinking about my baby and the mental anguish he's going through hurts me. Prada masks the shit so well.

"It's okay to be his safe place, sis. Just don't let that shit spiral out of control. Don't worry about me saying anything about this to G. Honestly, I think all of them niggas are fighting demons. Team Supreme is their façade to under-lying pain. They have immersed themselves into running shit, and they have yet to really deal with the fact that their mother was murdered behind this shit. That goes for Ms. Gladys too. That woman can't even talk about her own daughter without crying. Now their long-lost father is back and lurking around. Like Dream said, it's always some shit going on with this family."

"I agree. Shit, we aren't the only ones with a dysfunctional fucked up ass family. Let's get in here and deal with Cruella." We both laughed and got out of the car.

We grabbed each other's hand and walked up to the door. Without knocking, we simply walked inside. My mother never locked the door. Why she thought she couldn't get murdered in the suburbs was beyond me.

"I should have known this was some bullshit!" Miyani yelled.

"Considering the fact that you weren't invited!" my mother responded.

"Shut up, I invited her, and it's a good thing I did. Why would you invite me here?" I was fuming, looking at Mr. and Ms. Roebuck sitting in the living room.

"Calm down, Gavin. We need to talk before things get out of hand."

"Things are already out of hand. Where is your abusive, manipulating lying ass son? He's the only reason y'all old white asses could be here trying to meet up with my sister."

"You were right, Melissa. She is disrespectful and unruly!" Mr. Roebuck said.

"Fuck you and Melissa, nigga."

"What is this about?" I asked, irritated as fuck.

This is exactly what I get for feeling as if I need closure. You just have to be done with some situations with no explanation needed. This is one of those situations. As God is my witness, I'm done with this woman.

"We know that you have cut ties with Carlo. However, that has nothing to do with us. We want to see our grandson. As a matter of fact, we thought it was only fair that we talk face-to-face. This is for you."

Mrs. Roebuck handed me a manila envelope. Opening it, I realized that they were suing me for sole custody of my son.

"Let me see this bullshit!" Miyani yelled as she snatched the paperwork from my hand.

"Really, ma? Like you really tricked me here so they could serve me with custody papers. You hate me being with Prada so much that you would let someone take my child away from me!" I hated to let this bitch see me cry, but I couldn't believe this shit. I should have brought my gun and murdered these motherfuckers.

"Thank you, Melissa. Let Malcolm know we hope he gets better." Them white devils smirked and hurriedly walked out of the house. This bitch sat smoking a cigarette and sipping on Cognac like it was nothing.

"You are a sick, demented bitch! Where is my father?"

"Why are you here again? Did you forget our conversation regarding your father?" my mother asked as she laughed.

Miyani looked like she was about to attack her ass, so I quickly stood in between them.

"What the fuck is your problem? Why are you doing this?"

"Cause she's an evil ass bitch! Since we're here, let's lay it out there. Apparently, the man who I've grown up to think is my father is not. Tell her, Melissa. Tell Gavin what you told me."

Clearly, I had been left out of the loop about something.

"It's simple. Malcolm is not Miyani's father. I was already pregnant when I met him. Knowing what I know now, she should have been the child I gave up for adoption and not India."

My eyes widened, and my heart stopped for a moment.

"Wait a minute. What do you mean India? Are you talking about G's rat ass baby momma?"

"Yes, that's exactly who I'm talking about. India is my

daughter from a previous relationship. Actually, Miyani and India share the same father. Malcolm knows all about everything."

This woman was sitting here casually speaking as if she wasn't giving us life-altering news.

"Why would he allow us to grow up and not tell us this?"

"I'm sorry, Gavin and Miyani. I always wanted you to know, but I couldn't bring myself to tell you. I love both of you, and I apologize from the bottom of my heart."

My father had walked inside the room in his house clothes and on a cane. He looked like a dying old man. Just a couple of months ago, he looked healthy as an ox. Now he looks like he would be dying any day. This man just got re-elected as the Mayor of Chicago. There is no way he should be in such a dire condition.

"Daddyyyy! What is wrong with you?" I cried as I rushed over to him.

"The doctors don't know. In the last month or so, my health has declined. I'm in so much pain I don't know what to do. I'm so glad to see you girls here. Miyani, I want you to know that no matter what, you are my daughter. We may not share the same blood, but that means nothing to me. I am your father!"

Miyani rushed over to my father, and we all stood in the middle of the floor hugging. Of course, our mother didn't join in. As I held on to my father, he felt like nothing but skin and bones. Something was terribly wrong. My father was in so much pain and my mother seemed not to care. He was shaking uncontrollably and trying his best to stand.

"Daddy, we need to get you to a different physician," Miyani said.

"You're not taking my husband anywhere. His doctor

knows what he's doing. It's time for both of you to leave. You're upsetting him."

"Bitch, if you don't get your hands off of me, I'm going to fuck you up!" I pushed her ass so hard that she damn near flew across the room. Miyani was right beside me ready to pounce on her ass.

Before she could react, the doorbell rang. Instead of her coming back at me, she headed over to the door. Once she opened the door, I became so angry seeing India standing there with that same stupid ass smile as my mother.

"I need to sit down!" my father yelled. Before we could turn around and get to him, he had collapsed.

"Daddy!" I screamed. Both Miyani and I rushed to his side. He was having what looked like a seizure.

"This is why I didn't want you bitches at my house. Call the ambulance, India!"

"Okay, ma!"

Hearing her say that angered me. I couldn't react to either of these bitches. All I could do was cry on the floor beside Miyani as our father took his last breath. What had we done wrong for this shit to happen to us? This shit just happened so fast that I can't wrap my mind around this shit.

THE ENTIRE WEEK had been a blur. Today was my father's funeral, and I just wanted the day to be over. My sister or I had no hand in the preparations. We learned about his services by watching the news. He was the Mayor of Chicago, so it was national news. Our mother had been on TV playing the part of the grieving widow. What hurt me the most was that she left Miyani and me out of everything. However, India was right beside her. The shit wasn't right at all. India didn't know Malcolm Mills like Miyani and I did. No matter what, that man raised us. Melissa can do whatever she wants, but nothing will change that.

"The car is ready, babe."

"Okay. Can you help me zip my boots, please?"

As Prada kneeled to zip my boots, I begin to cry. Our relationship wasn't in the best place, and I needed it to be. With everything that was going on, I felt like he was slipping away from me too. Within the blink of an eye, I lost my parents. I would lose my mind if Prada stopped loving me. Call me a weak bitch I don't care. When a man comes into your life and loves you properly, you hold on to that shit. He has his flaws, but he's so good to my son and me.

"Come on now. Stop that." He reached up and wiped my tears.

"I'm sorry. I just feel like I'm losing everything. The Roebucks are trying to take my baby, my father is dead, and you're mad at me. I'm sorry about taking the birth control pills." Now I was crying like a damn fool. I'm sure Prada wanted to tell me to shut up with this ugly ass cry I was doing.

"You will never lose me unless God calls me home or them pigs take me! I love you, Gavin, and I'm not going no motherfucking where. You can believe that shit. As far as you taking birth control pills, that's your right as a woman. I had no right to be mad at you or in my feelings about the shit. Here, I was going to wait until all of this shit was over, but you need a little happiness this morning. Gavin Mills, will you marry me?"

I covered my face and just cried like a baby. Just to have some type of joy in the midst of mourning had me overwhelmed.

"Yes, I'll marry you, Prada Alexander!"

I grabbed him tightly by the face and kissed him passionately. I've always dreamed of one of those heartfelt proposals. Right now, I'm going to take what the hell I can get from this complicated man that I love so much.

"We will celebrate later. Right now, we need to go so that you and Miyani can pay your respects to your pops. Don't you worry about shit. Y'all got the whole Team Supreme locked, loaded, and ready for whatever."

Hearing Prada say that made me grab my gun and put it in my purse. After all, I am a part of Team Supreme, not to mention I'm not taking any chances where Melissa Mills is concerned. The bitch showed me exactly who she is this week, not that I didn't know before. It's just that it took my father to die for her to completely disown us. I'm wondering if the hoe is really my damn mother after all of this shit.

~

"I'm sorry, Ms. Gavin and Ms. Miyani, I can't let you in." A full damn security team was blocking the entrance of the church.

"Are you serious right now? You've been head of security since we were kids. You know he's our father."

I was in disbelief hearing what Braxton was saying. This man had been a part of our childhood. He was our personal driver for school at one point.

"I know that, but your mother has strict orders not to let either of you inside of the services."

This shit was so embarrassing. All the news stations were set up, and crowds of people were taking pictures of us.

"You know I hate to do this. I need my job, and Mrs. Mills will have it if I defy her orders.

"How about I put a bullet in your fucking head? Get the

fuck out of her way!" Prada had pulled his gun out and had it up to Braxton's head. That made the rest of the security team pull theirs out. Of course, Team Supreme had their shit out too.

"Mrs. Gladys, can you please calm your grandsons down? I don't want to arrest them."

"You won't have to arrest them if you let these girls in to pay their respects to their father. I don't pay you good enough, Owens? What? Is that bitch Melissa pay off bigger than mine?

"Don't forget who put them ugly ass daughters of yours through college!" Fendi said.

"I say we bum rush this motherfucker!" Nettie yelled!

"All of that isn't necessary. Put the guns away, and I'll let you all in. Just know Mrs. Mills is going to try to fight tooth and nail to keep you out."

"Well, she's going to have to fight us all because we in this bitch!" Miyani yelled.

"You are far too pretty for that type of language, Ms. Mills."

"That's a married woman. Show some motherfucking respect. Address her as Mrs. Alexander, my nigga! She's not pretty. She's beautiful, nigga!" Givenchy gritted as he stepped in front of everybody and stared down the officer.

The crazy part was that they weren't married yet. None of us had officially gotten married, but these niggas made people treat us like we were legally their wives. You see why I love being a part of Team Supreme.

"Get y'all fat asses out of our way!" Dream started pushing through the officers, and we managed to get inside the church.

The first person I locked eyes with was Carlo. Prada immediately grabbed my hand tight. I was so happy I decided to leave my son at home with Ms. Paulette. This man and his family were never going to see my son again.

"I know that ain't that hoe Esha!" Dream yelled.

This bitch had locked hands with Carlo. She winked her eye at me, and I snatched away from Prada. All I saw was blood as I tried to kill this bitch with my bare hands. Miyani, Dream, and Ms. Gladys had joined in. We were fucking her ass up good. I could feel people grabbing me, but they couldn't get us off the hoe.

"Beat that bitch's ass, and you bet not spare her! Step back, y'all. Let my baby do her thing. I'm going to shoot the first motherfucker that even thinks about grabbing her. Box them in Butta and Gunna. If anybody moves funny, shoot their ass!" I heard Prada yell, and I did exactly that.

I whipped that hoe's all up and down them church pews. It was pure pandemonium, and I didn't care. The bitch wasn't fighting back, so it was a waste of time to keep kicking her ass. She had balled up on the floor with her face covered.

"This is exactly why I didn't want them here! Look at how they behave at their own father's funeral."

"Aht Aht, bitch! Remember he's not my father," Miyani said.

"This is ridiculous! No wonder she wants nothing to do with either of you. Look how y'all behaving. It's a good thing we reunited with each other. It's obvious she needs a real daughter because neither of you knows what it takes to be one."

"Whoop her motherfucking ass right now, Miyani! G yelled.

My sister went full speed ahead, fighting her ass. Of course, India was fighting back. I quickly jumped in and started helping her. My mother tried to jump in, but Dream and Ms. Gladys started beating the fuck out of her. Before we knew it, all of our asses were in cuffs going to jail being charged with a slew of charges. The shit was so embarrassing but oddly satisfying as fuck. I'm still fucked up to learn that Esha was now with Carlo. She thinks I whipped her ass. He's going to be whipping that ass for breakfast, lunch, and dinner.

15

——————

PRADA

"We should have killed that bitch India the moment she popped back up. I knew some shit was not right with that bitch!" I heatedly said as I paced back and forth. The whole family was sitting in Team Supreme Headquarters, trying to figure out our next move.

After sitting in jail for damn near twenty-four hours, we had all been released. With all of us locked up, Silk was the only person we could call to get us out. The shit was crazy but funny at the same time. My grandma hates him so bad that she didn't even say thank you. The man had used his own bread and bonded all of our asses out. As far as Ms. Gladys was concerned, he owed us that money.

"Who would have known India would be sisters with Miyani and Gavin? That has to have you feeling some type of way, huh, G?" Nettie said.

"That bitch is not our sister! Please don't ever let those words come out of your mouth again, or I swear to God we will fall out!" Miyani spoke with an obvious attitude.

"I'm sorry, sis. It's just that this some Lifetime movie type of shit."

"To answer your question, I don't feel shit about it. When I first found out about the connection with them, I was shocked but not surprised."

"Wait a minute! What the fuck you mean when you found out about it? How long have you known about this, Givenchy!"

"Calm down, old lady! After all of these years of knowing me, y'all know how I move with certain things. My daughter's wellbeing was on the line, so I had to make sure I moved cautiously. Plus, Miyani and Gavin's safety was on the line as well. In case y'all forget their lives just changed forever. I know Team Supreme is our main priority, but right now, I want to focus on making sure they're good. After all, they did just get out of jail for fucking them snake ass bitches up at their father's funeral." G laughed, and it made all of us join in.

I grabbed Gavin and kissed her. She made a nigga proud as fuck the way she held her own.

"For you to be a ballerina, you have a mean ass right hook!" Fendi said.

"I tried to kill that bitch, India! The next time I catch that bitch, it's on sight and every time after that as well."

"Let's talk about Dream beating the hell out of Melissa. Who knew she looked like Fire Marshall Bill underneath all that damn horse hair?"

"Don't blame that on me, Ms. Gladys! You were walking that hoe like a dog!"

"They all had that shit coming. I'm just embarrassed that shit is headline news. It's as if my mother wanted to embarrass us and make India look good. I'm over all of this. That lady killed my father. I can't prove it, but I feel it inside of me. Thanks for having our back and being there for us today. We definitely couldn't have done it without Team Supreme. I love y'all, but I have to go home and lay it down. I'm exhausted." Gavin dabbed at the tears in her eyes, and I just felt my blood boiling.

"We're about to get up out of here. I'll get up with y'all tomorrow," I said as I dapped it with everybody and kissed my granny. Right now, I just needed to focus on trying to make my baby feel better.

~

WHEN WE MADE IT HOME, Gavin cried herself to sleep. A nigga couldn't even sleep knowing she was going through so much mental anguish.

It hurt my heart the way my baby was treated. Neither she nor Miyani deserve that shit, and it has me heated as fuck. It was so much deeper shit going on than what appeared at the service. It had to be. Givenchy always tells us it's important to use our brains instead of reacting. Everybody knows Fendi and me be war-ready around this motherfucker. I've been trying my best to stay level headed, but the shit that happened at that fucking funeral was a deal-breaker.

If a motherfucker thinks they're going to play with Gavin and not suffer behind it, they got the game fucked up. I'm all about my business, but the shit gets personal when I see my baby hurt. I have to defend her honor no matter what. Team Supreme has always been my main priority but right now, they come second. Gavin and CJ deserve to be protected. At this point, I'm all they have, and I intend on being here for them one hundred percent.

FENDI and I sat parked outside of Blackbird, an upscale restaurant where political figures in the city frequented. We were waiting for the Roebucks to come outside. I had been following their every move ever since Gavin told me about them serving her with the custody papers. They were creatures of habit. For them to be so damn rich and ruthless, they were dumb than a motherfucker. Even a hood nigga like myself knew it was essential to switch up the routine on a regular. Surprisingly, they never had security with them. Ruthless people like that should never leave home without protection. They believe that being white and privileged will grant them a pass. That shit means nothing to hood wolves like us. It makes them easy fucking prey. Motherfuckers couldn't keep walking around thinking they were about to take CJ from Gavin.

Glancing over at Fendi, I watched as he rubbed some Neosporin on his fucked up face.

"I've been meaning to ask you what the fuck happened to your ass?" The nigga looked like he had been in a damn catfight.

"I was fighting with Dream's crazy ass."

"Well, nigga, you definitely lost! What the hell did she do, bite your ass?" I couldn't help but laugh at him. Had it been me, the nigga would be going in on me nonstop, so I'm definitely enjoying this shit.

"Hell yeah! The shit still hurt like a motherfucker."

"Nigga, she got them damn plastic surgery teeth. I forgot what they be calling them bitches. All I know is they can cut through dinosaur bone. Your ass is about to get married to Hannibal Lector!"

"Fuck you, nigga! Let's get this shit over with. They just walked out of the restaurant."

We pulled the ski masks over our faces and hopped out of the car. Givenchy was going to be pissed when he finds out we made a move without him. We can deal with him later. This shit needed to be handled expeditiously! There was no time for his long, drawn-out speeches. Don't get me wrong. I love my brother's advice and the way he handles shit. It has saved us so many times. However, I just be wanting to murder shit and get it over with.

With precision Fendi and I casually walked up to Mr. and Mrs. Roebuck while they waited for the valet to bring their car around. They never knew what hit them as we dumped bullets in both of their bodies. People on the street didn't realize what the fuck had happened. The silencers we used suppressed the sound of the gunshots. Screaming in the distance could be heard as we pulled away from the crime scene. We did the shit sweet as fuck. It will definitely go down in history for how brazen we were.

I headed home once we burned our clothes, had the car chopped up, and had gotten rid of the guns. A nigga had been gone since early in the morning. I'm surprised Gavin hadn't been blowing my phone up talking shit.

Jumping on the highway to head home, I received a text from Silk asking me to meet up with him. This nigga had been calling for the last two days. I had been trying my best to ignore him because I wasn't trying to get caught up with his ass. A part of me still didn't trust him. All of these years, he was always the perfect scapegoat to pin my mother's murder on. After he explained things to us, I'm almost positive he wasn't the triggerman.

All this new information had me back popping Percocet like candy. I was reliving what I saw all those years ago. I remember the person who shot my mother had on these black and gold pinky rings. If I ever saw it again, I would know it. It's embedded in my memory bank. I just wished I would have stayed instead of running away. When she was in the chest she instantly went down. The shock of seeing it caused me to panic and piss on myself. I was eight years old and the shit fucked me up to the point where I couldn't tell anyone.

Silk's ass just wasn't letting up, so I told him to drop a location, and I would meet him there. The whole ride over to where he wanted to meet up, I tried to process the fact that Silk was very much back around. It was hard for me to see him as the man who is my father. The only memories I have of him is beating my mother's ass. The way I feel this nigga is lucky I don't put a bullet in his head when I meet up to see what the fuck he wants.

"WHAT'S GOOD?" I asked as I got inside of Silk's Benz.

For this nigga to have just got out of federal prison, he was holding. He bonded all of us out with no problem and never asked for the bread back, not that we were going to pay his ass anyway. I'm just wondering how much of that old school money he stashed away before he went behind the wall.

"Thanks for coming. I wish Fendi and G would have answered for me. I'm grateful that you did."

I observed him reaching inside of a secret compartment and grabbing his Glock.

"What you on, OG?"

"You strapped?"

"I keep my bitch on me. Now tell me what the fuck is

going on?" This nigga was looking like he was here to do a fucking job. I had just gone done murking some people.

"You see that house right there. That's where that nigga Butch is hiding out at. I reached out to some of my old people and found out this is where he traps at. Sit back! Somebody is pulling up!"

Both of us fell back a little and watched as a black Cadillac truck pulled into the driveway.

"What the hell are them bitches doing here?" It shocked me looking at Melissa and India get out of the car.

"I don't know who the younger chick is, but the older bitch is Madam Mink. That's Butch's bottom bitch. Back in the day, she ran one of the most lucrative prostitution rings Chicago had ever seen. I was shocked to get out and learned she had married the damn mayor. Look, the bitch still up to her old tricks."

My eyes widened seeing her pull two women from the backseat of the truck. They were clearly being held against their will. They had handcuffs and shackles on their ankles. I didn't even bother to go into detail about Melissa or the fact that she was Miyani and Gavin's mother. Right now, I was ready to go inside and kill them bitches. It was the perfect opportunity to get rid of their ass.

"Let's fall off in there and see what's good. It's obvious they're holding bitches against their will."

"You think we should try getting in contact with your brothers? I think it's important we all get a chance to question that nigga in regard to what happened to Chanel."

"We don't have time. Let's handle this shit and get the fuck out of dodge."

Melissa and India roughly pushed the two women as they all walked inside of the garage. Luckily, for us, they forgot to close the door. Silk and I slowly crept inside of the garage. I swear these were some of the stupidest criminals I've ever seen. They had made some rookie ass mistakes. They hadn't locked the door that led from the garage to the inside of the house.

"If any of these motherfuckers act like they want smoke, give it to them!" Silk spoke through gritted teeth. He didn't have to tell me because I already had it in my mind that I was killing them.

As we walked inside the house, I could hear Melissa's aggravating ass voice. It was about to be the highlight of my life putting a bullet in the bitch's head. We stopped and listened to her conversation.

"Why the fuck would you bring them here? I don't need that heat over here."

"Really, Butch! Have you been watching the news? The Roebucks were gunned down tonight outside of Blackbird. I know them motherfuckers coming for us next. I just need to lay low here until my pilot can get us to the Dominican Republican. I have buyers for them over there. They've already sent the deposit. All I have to do is get them sold, and I'm in the clear. No one will ever know about this shit!"

"I can't believe you've been holding Chanel and her daughter hostage all of these years. I should never have let you talk me into this shit."

"You should have thought about that before you started fucking her. It's not my fault your aim is off and she survived!

"No! What you should have done was left her in the hospital in the coma? Her sons are going to murder y'all ass when they found out what you did. That janky ass hospital and the government all had a hand in her kidnapping. All I want to do is have a relationship with my daughters Miyani and India! I didn't sign up for this other shit.

"What the fuck?" I said in a low tone.

The wheels in my head started to turn as I rushed through the house, trying to find the women they had just brought in the house.

"Slow down, Prada!" I could hear Silk say behind me, but I couldn't stop. Seeing India step out of a room made me jump back so that she wouldn't see me. Once she was out of sight, I rushed to the door and opened it. I fell to my knees, looked at my mother chained to the other woman. I didn't know if this was a nightmare or a dream come true.

"This shit can't be real!"

"What have they done to you, ma?" I moved her hair from her face and she locked eyes with me.

"Prada baby, is that you?"

!!TO BE CONTINUED!!

LETTER FROM THE AUTHOR

I had all intentions to end this book with just two parts. However, so many readers reached out to me and asked me to do another part. I never anticipated Hood Supreme to be such a popular series. I've received so much feedback on these characters. It was only right I give the majority more than two books. Part 3 will definitely be the Finale of this series. Thank you all so much for making this book series so a success!!!!!!!

9 798667 973812